B.D.PEDERSEN

Duker's Store

Edited by

June Pedersen

ISBN-13: 978-0692416068
ISBN-10: 0692416064

Prologue

Duker's Store, every city or town has a store just like Duker's. A place where one can go and find just about anything they need. The only difference is Duker's Store was a place where people went to find whatever it was, they needed to complete their life's dream.

The problem with Duker's is it made no difference what that dream was, ugly, good, or bad, they could find whatever it was to fulfill their needs there at Duker's Store.

Delbert Millhouse made his way to Duker's one day in search of a few answers to the questions he had about Duker's Store and where it came from. He had been researching the store and found little or no information on the store itself or the person who created it and the persons who ran it or worked there.

Delbert would enter the store just as so many before him, the only difference being he would never exit it. What would happen to Delbert in that store over the next few hours would change the whole of his life and send him down a whole new path.

As Delbert entered the store, Frank Duker was standing there to meet Him. Frank was a friendly sort and offered his hand as Delbert entered. At that moment Delbert had a feeling this man was going to be taking him for a rather interesting trip through the store, a trip that would ultimately end with him retiring and leaving Delbert with the store lot, stock and barrel.

It's not that Delbert wanted the place or that he was looking to own it in the first place. He wasn't, all he wanted was information, that's all. He was curious about the store and its history and having failed to find anything of any substance elsewhere he went to the store to see if he could get the information he wanted.

Instead what Delbert ended up with was a trip through time and the introduction of what the store was actually all about. He would learn the store was much more than he had ever thought.

Maybe it would be better if he let you find that out, as he did. Just remember Duker's Store is not your average store. It is far more than that and the stories presented here will give you a clear understanding of Duker's Store and what it is really all about.

Delbert could tell that as he heard the stories he watched Frank and paid particularly close attention to his demeanor and mannerisms. All Delbert could say was that Frank was dedicated and clearly a good man. It would be this man who would walk Delbert through the issue of accepting the fact he was now the new owner of Duker's Store.

Delbert learned life was made up of all types of people and each one had their own path they were following through their lives. Life is made up of the good and the bad. It's made up of people making personal decisions they will live and die by. Decisions that will change their lives, some for the good and some for the bad, some will find their lives changed in ways they would have never believed.

Delbert was to learn he would have to keep his feelings and interests separated from customer's dreams and actions. In the end each individual would do as they must and there is nothing he or anyone else can do about it.

When they enter the store, they have a need and the store will provide for that need, whatever it may be. Yet there are rules, and one is whatever they do they cannot use some items as the means of hurting or killing another human being. That too would result in some rather unusual events that even the person who came to the store had not expected.

It's understood just about anything can be used to harm other, but some things are dedicated to harm and they could not be use as such. Anything else would involve the desires and actions of the person using the item in question.

Duker's Store is a place where people go one at a time for their own particular reason or purpose. Yes only one person can be in Duker's Store at any given time. That's the reason for the single parking spot in front of the store. They would drive up and park in that one spot and then enter the store many times not understanding why they are there.

For whatever reason, they needed something, some particular item and they ended up there at Duker's Store. The only place on the face of the earth they could find that one particular item or items that would fulfill their needs and their path in life. The only place where time does not matter, where time is the same for those from the past, those from the future and those from the now have an equal footing to work from.

Chapter One

Delbert Millhouse

Anyone who has grown up in and around Brownsville knows about Duker's Store. It's been a landmark in these parts for at least a hundred year, maybe more. It has always been in the same place, dead center on Main Street, with the same front and same paint color in all that time.

I'm not sure just what kind or type of store it was; I guess you would call it a General Store. But if you asked ten different people the type store it was they would give you ten different answers. The one thing about Duker's was no matter what you wanted or needed you could find it at Duker's.

Believe me when I tell you if you want a horseshoe, they had them in every size you could think of. If you wanted quilting materials, they had a selection that made the big box stores look like pikers. No matter what it was, this store had it. I could never figure that out. Whenever I walked into the place, I knew what I wanted was there waiting for me.

Another thing that stood out, I never saw more than one clerk in the store at any time and it was always the same clerk. I don't care what day of the week it was; the same clerk was there.

He was an older man, maybe in his mid-fifties, with a balding head, glasses and an eye shade on his head. He always met you or me at the front door of the store and would ask what I needed.

During that time I thought nothing of it. It was just the clerk, probably the owner, and he was giving me the service he felt I should have. No matter what I asked him he had an answer and it was always the right one. I didn't think about it, I just went and got what I needed and left and went home to do whatever it was I was doing. I never thought about the store and its location, the clerk, the décor, the single parking spot in front, or anything else about the place.

If I was going to Duker's, for whatever reason, I would drive down Main Street and if the parking spot was taken I would continue on and forget about my need until later. It never occurred to me there was never more than one car parked in front of the store.

It was years later when I was sitting at home one day reading the newspaper when I came by an article title, "Owner of Duker's Store looking for new owner." In all the years that store had been there that is the first time I saw the name Duker's Store in the paper. In fact, there had never been an ad run in any paper in all the years Duker's had been there, never.

That caused me to set back and start to think about Duker's, I mean I really started to think about the store and its history in our town. It overwhelmed me as I thought about the store; I needed to learn more all the while I sat there. Finally I got up and went out to my car and headed for the library. If there's one place around here that will have any history on Duker's, this would be the place.

Once at the library I was at a loss as to where to start my search. I knew my subject and so I went to the librarian and asked. "Where can I find any history on Duker's Store?"

She looked at me and then stood back. "You want information on Duker's Store?"

"Yes, I have been thinking about that place for a while and then read the news article about the store in this morning's paper. It's up for sale you know."

She stood there looking at me. "Well, I guess the best place to start is in the old files on the city's development and growth. You can find those files over in the City Heritage Section, there behind you on the second shelf."

I thanked her and walked over to the shelf she pointed out and found the files on the history of Brownsville. As I sat down and opened the file I found the paperwork on the founding of Brownsville. There where pictures of the location or area where the city had been proposed and then more photos of the development of Main Street. One of the first pictures of Main Street had one building sitting on the street and that was Duker's Store. No lie, there it was, a picture, the first known picture of the store and Brownsville's Main Street that was two hundred thirty-five years ago.

I looked at the picture and set it aside I flipped through several more pictures until I came to a second one that was three years later. There were several more small stores on the street but Duker's was still there and looked exactly the same as it does now.

I continued going through the history of the city and when I got to the end, I remembered I had seen nothing else on Duker's Store. Those first two pictures were the only pictures or reference to Duker's Store. That seemed strange to me. So far I had found just those two things and nothing else.

It then came to me I needed to track the name Duker. Where did it come from and how many Duker's' were there. I turned to the computer and entered a search for the name Duker. I sat there waiting for the listing to come up. Strange, it was taking a long time to come up with any files and that told me there were a lot of files on the Duker family and I needed to wait.

Finally the screen came to life and up popped a single entry on the name Duker. I sat there looking at it. The machine had taken five minutes and it came up with one name for Duker. That name was Frank, Frank Duker. That was it. There were no additional files or references, just the name Frank Duker. I waited thinking files on Frank would be following and nothing came.

I had been here fifty-five minutes and all I had was two pictures of the store and the name of the apparent owner and nothing else. I was perplexed and had no idea as to where to go next. So, when in doubt, always go to the librarian and that's what I did.

I walked up to the counter and she turned to me. "Yes sir can I help you?"

I stood there a moment. "I'm not sure if you can or not. You see I have been doing a little research on the Duker's Store down on Main Street. My problem is all I can find are two pictures of the store and the name Frank Duker. I was wandering if you could assist me in finding out more information on the Store and Mr. Duker?"

By this time she was smiling. "No that's all we have on the store. I have often wondered myself why so little information was available on that place. I have never been able to find anything else out about the store or the Duker family.

"May I suggest this to you? Have you thought about going to the store and talking to the clerks there? Maybe they have all the information you would need right there in the store."

Hell of an idea, I stood there thinking. Yeah, if they don't have it here then the only place to go is to the source and that was the store. I thanked the lady and turned to leave. She called out to me. "Oh by the way the clerks name is Frank. I just thought you may want to know."

What the hell was going on here anyway? Now I was on my way over to Duker's Store to contact the clerk there and as it turns out his name is Frank too. There was something funny going on and I had to pursue it. There was no other way around it, I had to go and I had to find out.

So far I had two pictures of the store and one name, probably the store owner. It dawned on me I found nothing on other employees or people who had worked there. That wasn't right, a store of its size, not really large, but not really small either, should have more than one employee. Come to think of it I couldn't find anything on the Duker family, where they lived and how large a family they were.

In all my years living here in Brownsville I realized there were no little Duker's running around or attending schools or playing in sports or anything for that matter. Odd, that had never entered my mind before. As far as I could tell anything having to do with Duker's was there, on main street, in that store and no place else.

By the way, my name is Delbert Millhouse. I was born in Brownville some thirty-one years ago and have lived here all my life. I have never left the town except for a few vacations I took with my parent and sibling way back when. As for myself, I have traveled but usually not more than two to three weeks at a time. Other than that, this is my life from the beginning and probably to the end.

I'm six feet tall and weigh in at two hundred pounds. I have red hair and green eyes and I love to run. That keeps me in fairly good shape because my normal work finds me sitting a lot. I'm an accountant at the local bank. I have a degree in accounting I obtained through an internet extension course out of the State University.

As people go, I'm your quintessential average Joe. I have never done anything special in my life having chosen to live a quiet and none descripted life. In other words, I'm a no body. And, why the hell do I have this thing about Duker's Store? What the hell am I trying to discover or find out?

So, here I am going over to Duker's Store to try and learn more about the history of the store and how it managed to keep in business this long, especially when it only has one parking place in front of the store, that's it, just one.

As I arrived at the store ten minutes later I started to wander about the single parking stall in front of the store. There was ample space for more stalls, but the rest of the street in front of the store was painted yellow making it a no parking zone.

Another thing, no one seemed to care or consider the fact there was only one parking place and the rest of the street in front of the store was painted as a yellow no parking zone. No one seemed to care one way or the other. Never, and I mean never, have I heard of any one questioning the layout in front of Duker's.

As I turned on to Main Street I could see a car parked in the single stall and drove on by and down to the next parking place available. I parked and got out of the car and started to walk back to the store. When I got to the door and tried to open it, I found it was locked. You heard me, the damn door was locked. How could anyone do business when they had only one customer and the door was locked to all other customers?

I turned and started to walk away and the door opened and Mary Spencer stepped out. "Hi Delbert, Frank is ready for you now."

I guess my mouth fell open or something because she started to laugh and held the door open for me. I stepped into the store and when the door closed I reached over and tried to open it. It opened no problem at all.

Yes, I've been here before to find things I needed for a particular problem or need. I never thought about the front door being locked while I was there shopping. In fact, I'm not sure it was actually locked when I walked up to it. She had said he had been waiting for me.

I then turned and there was Frank standing just three feet from me. "Hi Delbert how are things?"

That wasn't normal. He usually said "May I help you?"

Right then I was a little lost for word but managed to regain my composure after a few seconds. "Hi Frank, you knew I was coming?" As I pointed back at the door I had just come through.

He was nodding his head. "Yes I knew you went to the library this morning to do some research on the store and myself. Did you find anything?"

How the hell did he know that? "Yeah, I found two pictures and a story about you. I had seen the ad in the paper that you were selling the store and it made me curious about the history of the store. Has anyone else approached you about buying the store?"

"Delbert, are you thinking of buying Duker's?"

That stopped me short again. "I didn't say that?"

"No you didn't but you asked if anyone else had approached me about buying the store. That told me you were interested in buying. Am I right?"

21

Right then, right that second I realized he was right. Why else would I do what I've been doing all morning? I looked at him and leaned back against the door. "I guess your right about that. I really didn't think it was for that reason but when I think about it, yes I am interested."

Frank walked up to me and took my left elbow in his right hand and pulled and led me toward the back of the store. He was walking slowly taking his time and preparing to say something, what, I really didn't know. "Delbert, I have watched you over the years and had known when the time came you would be the one person to show the greatest interests in my store. The fact is Delbert I will be leaving here shortly and I want to ensure the right person takes over my store.

"So, if you don't mind I would like to go over the history of Duker's Store and give you a better understanding as to just what the store is to the community and to individual people who live here in Brownsville.

"To start with, Duker's was built on this site twenty years before Brownsville was incorporated. We provided service to the farmers who lived in the area and managed to maintain a good relationship with all those people over the years. We've all shared a lot over these many years.

"The store was originally built by my grandfather Adolf Duker and I eventually took it over. My father was lost to us shortly after I was born so grandfather maintained the store until I was old enough to run the store."

I had raised my hand when he got that far. "How long did your grandfather run the store?"

By this time we were approaching the office at the back of the store. Frank reached out to open the door and then turned toward me. "He ran the store for seventy-seven years. When I took over, I was thirty-one years old."

That shut me up fast, if Frank's grandfather had run the store seventy-seven years, and the store as two hundred thirty-five years old, that means Frank had been running this store for one hundred fifty-eight years. I felt my face flush and I reached out and took hold of the door jam. Frank stepped toward me and steadied me as I tried to deal with the fact, he had been running the store for a hundred fifty-eight years.

Impossible, it was just simply impossible that he was that old. If he took over the store at age thirty-one and he ran the place for a hundred fifty-eight years that would make him one hundred eighty-nine years old. Bull shit, no ones that old in this time and age. The Bible referred to Methuselah being somewhere around eight hundred years old, but that was before the flood. No one lived that old now.

Frank kept smiling at me and nodding his head. "You've figured it out haven't you Delbert. Yes, I'm a hundred eighty-nine years old and it's time for me to move on and do something else.

"My problem is I need someone who can take over the store and keep it running. Do you think you're that someone?"

All right, hold everything, I need to go back home and go into my bedroom and crawl back into my bed and wake up the right way. This was all wrong and I had to be dreaming, no I was having a nightmare. Man I've never dreamed like this before and I was beginning to believe my own dream.

"Delbert, you're not dreaming. What is happening here is actually happening. You have shown an interest in Duker's Store and that qualifies you as the most logical choice for taking over the store. It's not a case of two, three or four people applying. The fact is

24

the first one to show interest is the one the store will go to. Delbert you're the first."

No, wait this can't be happening. I don't know how to run a store. Damn, I'm doing the best I can just keeping up with my accounting work. A store! No way in hell. "Frank I just came to ask you some questions not buy your store. I don't know anything about running a store."

He was now smiling bigger than ever. He led me into his office and pointed at a chair for me to sit in. He moved around behind his desk and sat down. We sat there looking at one another for several seconds. My head was swimming and I could feel the sweat running down my back. I had started out on a simple research project and now I'm on the brink of buying Duker's Store.

Again, Frank sat there smiling at me as I wrestled with the proposition of becoming a store owner. He leaned toward me. "Delbert, you are not going to be buying the store. The store will be given to you and you will operate it as it has been operated over the past two hundred thirty-five years. You will live a good life and a most interesting one as well. You will welcome one customer at a time to your store and then provide them with whatever it is they want or need.

"Delbert, many of your customers will have no idea as to what it is they want. In fact they will have no idea as to why they came to this store in the first place. They will come through the front door looking for an answer and you will be the one to give it to them.

Sometimes it will solve their problem and other times it will aggravate it or make it more complex. It all depends on the customer, their situation at the time and what they are trying to do to cope with their problem.

"You will learn to enjoy the many situations men and women can get themselves into. Sometimes they come out good and sometimes bad. There is nothing you can do about it. All you can do is give them whatever it is they are in need of or think they are in need of. From then on fate takes the wheel and life moves on."

All right, I'm not dreaming, but I need to find a way out of this and find it now. If what Frank was saying was all true, then it's probably is a good life, but it's not the life for me and I needed out right now. "Look Frank I think I understand what you're trying to do, but you've found the wrong guy for the job.

I'm not cut out for this kind of work and besides I know nothing about it."

He sat there looking at me with this kind of wise smile on his face. He waited patiently for me to finish and then brought his hands up to his chin and sat there rocking back and forth. "Delbert life is filled with strange things, wouldn't you agree?"

I had to give him that one. "Yes I agree."

"At times we think we know what's about to happen and if we had truly taken a long hard look at the situation we would know it for sure. Would you agree to that?"

"Yes, I would agree with you on that as well."

"Since you left home this morning you had set out to try and find as much information on Duker's Store you could. In your pursuit of that goal you finally ended up here at the store."

"Yes again, but I was looking only for information as a means of satisfying my curiosity."

"True you were doing just that. The question is Delbert, why did you suddenly have a desire to know as much as you could about Duker's Store?"

That one got me. I had no idea as to why this subject had gotten into my mind and drove me to such lengths I finally came here in search of an answer. "I guess over the years I have developed a desire to know about the store. I've seen and heard so many stories about the store I finally wanted to know if they were actually true. Everyone in these parts has had the same feelings and thoughts as I have."

"Yes Delbert, many have, but you were the only one to follow through. You took direct steps to learn the truth about the store and all the stories that have come from this place.

"Well Delbert, those desires are about to be proven successful. Those desires were responsible for bringing you to this point in time. We are at a point when a new owner and operator of this store must step in and take over the operation of the store.

"Before that could happen, the right person needed to come through that door and into this store. This person would come through the door not needing anything physical but needing something that was intangible and indescribable. He would be looking for the life's blood of this store and the family who ran it for all these two hundred thirty-five years. Delbert, that person was you.

"Never in all the two hundred thirty-five years of this store's existence has there been anyone whoever entered this store seeking information on the store and not on a physical need such as a tool, or plumbing supplies.

Whether you realize it or not, you have been selected by the will of time to step into this place and take it over. Delbert, it has nothing to do with what you want and everything to do with what is going to happen."

Now I was really scared. This thing was getting out of hand and I knew I had to get up and get the hell out of there. I stood up and walked over to the door and opened it. I turned back to Frank. "Look I don't know what's going on here and I'm telling you here and now I'm not interested. I don't want to hear any more about this and please do not contact me in any manner from here on."

I walked out of the office and through the store to the front door and opened it and stepped out onto the street. I turned and closed the door and then turned again and found myself standing inside the store. I again grabbed the door knob and opened the door and stepped out onto the street and took one step away from the door and found myself back inside the store.

Frank was standing there watching me go through this exercise of futility. "Delbert, I'm sorry you feel that way but my hands are tied. You've been selected and there's nothing I or you can do about it. Duker's Store is now yours and you will live here in this store for as long as time deems you should be here."

I felt the hopelessness wash over me as Frank walked up to me and took me by my left elbow and led me back to his office. "Delbert, sit down and let me tell you a story. In fact I want to tell you several stories and hopefully this will make your adaptation to this reality that much easier."

I sat there and watched as he walked around to the other side of the desk. I was spent and sick at the same time. I felt like a bird in the grip of a small child not knowing what will come of me as this creature held me close to its face and looked at and wondered of the marvel of this small feathered creature.

"Delbert, I can assure you this is a great job and life. It is rich in the memories of the people who live in this part of the state, here in Brownsville. As I think back, I remember the funny, the sad, the weird, and the terror people have been facing when they enter this store and leave not knowing they had been directed on to the path they needed to take in order to bring their lives to fruition.

"Please, sit back and let me tell you of some of the more interesting cases that have passed through this place. Maybe that will help you understand what this is all about, what Duker's Store really is? Delbert I want you to meet eleven people and their stories and relationship with Duker's Store."

Chapter Two

Harvey 'Dinky' Sandburg

"Delbert, you must understand what a person does with their life is that person's responsibility. Yes, people can fall victim to someone else's actions, but for the most part we are all responsible for our own actions.

Then you have the person come along who doesn't have the slightest idea what responsibility is and how it impacts their life. This story is one that clearly demonstrates a person living within his own limited understanding of himself and life in general. As a result he will pay for it.

...Dinky Sandburg was a regular guy. He grew up in Brownsville on the north side of town. His parents were hard working and provided a good home for Dinky and his four brothers and sisters. I don't know where he got the name Dinky I just know that's what everyone called him. Few people knew his first name was Harvey.

Dinky had a habit that seemed to never clear up for him. He was always getting himself into some kind of trouble. Not with the law or anything like that, I mean trouble like forgetting he was working on scaffolding and turning and walking off into thin air.

If anything strange or mind boggling were to happen to anyone it would be Dinky. One time he was at the grocery store and on his way out he saw old Miss. Jenkins carrying her groceries out to her car. He ran over to help her and when he offered to help she looked at him like he was some kind of a monster.

"No" she said as she tried to push her way past him, but Dinky was a spunky sort and he refused to be rebuffed. He tried to take the groceries from her arms and she gave him a push and as he fell back he grabbed the top of the bag and took it with him. Now old

Miss. Jenkins wasn't going to be out done by the likes of this impetuous creature and she hung on for dear life.

Well Dinky went down on his back and the bag of groceries came down on top of him followed closely by Miss. Jenkins. They both hit the ground at the same time and when they did it sandwiched the bag of groceries between them. The first thing out of the bag was a carton of eggs and they landed right on Dinky's chest followed closely by Miss. Jenkins head.

There was enough force to cause the carton to split and dump a dozen eggs onto Dinky's chest, his neck and up onto his face. Right behind that came an exploding bottle of molasses and behind that a two pound bag of flour. Of course all during this time Miss. Jenkins was trashing around on top of him trying to get off and away from the maniac who had attacked her.

All that moving around managed to ensure every egg was broken and the eggs flour and molasses were completely mixed together along with a box of Cheerios and a bag of rice.

Miss. Jenkins finally ended up sitting on the ground next to Dinky, looking at the mess she was sitting in and the mess that was sitting alongside her. Dinky started to say something when she ended the conversation with a blow to the side of his head with her purse.

Dinky was always finding himself in some self-made situation. But the topper would be the one he found himself in on the 3rd day of July 1978. It was one of those hot July 4th weekends, the temperature was scorching and it hadn't rained for almost a month.

He was the type of guy who was always looking for shortcuts, ways of doing things that would save him time and make the job much easier. On this particular day I saw him pull up and park in front of the store. I was standing at the door when he came in. He seemed to be in good spirits and was looking around. "Dinky, what can I do for you?"

"Hi, Frank. Hey I need some dynamite, do you carry any here?"

Now in this business you never ask a person why they want something. That is not your right to know, all you do is supply them with whatever it is they want. "Why yes Dinky I have a case right over here on the counter just waiting for you."

35

He turned, looking out the front door window and then turned back to me. "I'll take the whole case Frank."

"My pleasure Dinky, you know a case of dynamite is expensive?"

"Don't worry Frank I have the money but I need a case right now."

"All right Dinky that will be $986.35 for one case of twenty-four sticks."

He looked at me like I was crazy. "God, I had no idea it was that expensive, how much for half a dozen sticks?"

"Sorry Dinky I can't break the case up, it's the whole case, all or nothing."

He stood there several seconds and then reached into his pocket and pulled out a wad of bills the likes of which I had never seen before. He counted out ten one hundred dollar bills and handed them to me.

I recounted the bills and then walked over to the counter and till. "All right Dinky there's your case of dynamite, please be careful carrying it out to your car and don't go throwing it around, understand? Now what do you want to use to set it off, caps or fuses?"

He thought for a few seconds. "Caps are too dangerous so I had better take fuses with me. I'll make sure they are long enough so I have time to get out of the way."

I set a pack of fuses on the case and he picked it up and turned from the counter. He again looked out the window and then at me and walked over to the door. I opened the door for him and he left. I watched as he placed the case in the trunk of his car and then got in and drove off down the street.

Now for me that was the end of the story, but for Dinky it was only the beginning. Dinky lived on a five acre plot on the north side of town. Out behind his house, about fifty yards away, was a huge oak tree that had been there for umpteen years and he had decided he was going to take it down.

You know Dinky; if he can think of a way to get out of any hard labor he will do it. So in comes the case of dynamite. It was the 4th of July weekend and Dinky thought that any additional noise around the area wouldn't be noticed. He drove on home and took the box of dynamite out of the car and took it out to the tree.

Now any normal person would cut the tree down and then cut it up into fire wood or furniture wood, whatever. But not Dinky he didn't like chain saws and he would never use a bucking saw for any reason. So he got a shovel and went to work digging out around the roots of the tree. He figured he didn't have to dig that much. All he needed was to be able to put the case of dynamite under the tree, set the fuse, and get the hell out of the way.

Sounded good, so he kept digging until he had the hole large enough to place the case into and then under the root system. He broke the case open and pulled a couple of sticks out and fused them up. He then placed them back into the case and ran the fuse out about fifteen feet from the case.

He looked around making sure there were no others present or nearby. He then struck a match and set the fuse off. After waiting until he was sure the fuse was going he turned and ran back to his house and stood on the back deck to watch the action.

He could see the fuse burning from where he was at when it dropped out of sight into the hole and he waited for the explosion to take place. Twenty four sticks of dynamite should put that tree down without any problem. If everything went right it should split every root and leave him with just the tree laying on the ground ready to be cut up for use.

Nothing was happening and he was sure he had set the fuse up right and so he waited. He started to think maybe he should go out there and check the charge to see if the fuse went out. No that would be foolish and what if he got out there and it went off in his face. He would wait.

He had no sooner gotten that thought out of his mind when there was an eruption out of the hole at the base of the tree like nothing he had seen before. Three things happened almost at the same time. First came the shock of seeing the blast, and then came the concussion wave that hit him and knocked him to the ground. Finally when the noise and concussion wave hit the house all the windows in the back of his house were blown in.

As Dinky sat there looking at the tree he saw it start to rise out of the hole and continue to rise higher and higher. As it went up it was starting to break apart into a number of pieces all of which were huge in comparison to Dinky and his body. He couldn't believe what he was looking at as the remains of that old Oak continued to climb into the sky.

Then he noticed they started to arch as they continued to accelerate. It didn't take him long to determine by the way they were arcing they were in fact coming directly toward his house. He jumped to his feet and started to run toward the hole in the ground and then stopped and reversed his direction and started to run for his house.

He got through the sliding glass doors on the patio into the house when the first part of the tree hit. It landed directly in the middle of the deck followed closely by the next large piece that hit the sliding glass door and drove itself into the house, catching Dinky half way across the living room and driving his body into the wall on the opposite side of the room from the door.

The third piece hit the roof and drove itself through and into the middle of the living room blowing a hole in the floor and burying itself in the ground under the house.

The fourth, fifth and sixth pieces picked the rest of the house apart leaving a pile of broken lumber, windows, doors, flooring, roofing, siding and various other parts of the house strewn all over the lawn and driveway.

When the fire department arrived they found the hole in the back yard and the tree on

40

Dinky's house and there in the middle of the destruction stood Dinky's lifeless body held up by several timbers that had fallen in on him pinning him in an upright standing position…

Now after hearing that story you may say I held part of the responsibility for Dinky's death because I supplied him with the dynamite he used and while using it he was killed. That's not the case. Dinky had determined before he entered the store what he was going to do. It is not my place to question any ones reasoning or decisions concerning their lives. That is each and every person's responsibility. First and foremost Dinky was responsible for his own actions no matter how outlandish they were.

As the proprietor of the store, I receive the information of the need for any number of items who people are going to come in and buy. It's not for me to question. I learned that lesson a long time ago. The order comes in and I fill it, that's all there is to it.

I have no choice even if I know what is going to happen and I had the opportunity to stop it. That Delbert is the nature of Duker's Store. You will learn this in time. Try as you may you cannot refuse to fill any and all orders or requests that come to Duker's Store.

The case of Dinky was sad and funny at the same time. Yet it tells a story that has meaning to it. It's a story of a person's laziness and the unreasonable ends he will go to in order to avoid a few hours of hard work. He looked for the biggest rock in the pile and when he used it he died by it. That my friend is life, in Dinky's case the end of his life. Not all issues of this nature end in the loss of one's life.

In the past two hundred thirty-five years this store has seen every kind of person and every kind of act pass through that door. You have noticed there is only one parking spot in front of this store. You have also discovered only one customer can be in the store at a time. In all those years no one has asked.

Why the hell just one parking spot and one customer at a time? That is until you came along and you asked the question. Delbert, in the process of asking you sealed your fate. It can be no other way.

Just as Dinky took a specific path in his life you have done the same. Dinky's decision was one of stupidity but yours was one of curiosity. The stupid decision ended in Dinky's death, your decision has resulted in your living for as long as you desire.

I had sat there listening to the story and wondering why anyone would do something as stupid as what Dinky had done. Yet I knew Dinky and he was that way. I understood why he died and it all made sense to me. He had always been that way, that was Dinky. I remembered the day when the news came out of his death. It was shocking but as the details of how he died became known he became the laughing stock of all of Brownsville.

If I were to be honest about it that was Dinky's destiny, if he hadn't died in that situation he would have in some other just as stupid and moronic act. I remembered his jet car. That was one time when I couldn't understand how he came out alive. He should have died that day but he didn't.

He was just past his eighteenth birthday and he had bought his first car. The truth is it was almost a car. Everything was there, most of it stuffed into the front and back seats. He had great plans for that car and told everyone someday, not too far down the road, he would drive that car through town

43

and everyone would know he was good to his word and a master mechanic.

The car disappeared into his father's barn as did Dinky. I didn't know what he was planning nor did anyone else, so we all let it pass figuring in the end his dad would have to truck that pile of junk out of the barn and off to the dump. Little did we know Dinky would be coming out of the barn in a way we could never have guessed.

Anyway, as time passed we all forgot about Dinky and his car and his great plans. I think it was around a year and half later that Dinky passed the word around his car was done and he would be driving it into town that coming Friday night. That was cool. People all over town were talking and planning on being on Main Street that night to get a look at Dinky's car.

It was a three day wait and finally Friday night came. I doubted if anyone would be there but there were a lot of people. What we didn't know was, we would be witnessing something so outlandish we would spend weeks trying to cope with it. It was ten after seven when we heard him coming. How do I describe what we witnessed? First of all was the noise. It sounded like a thunder storm coming at us.

Everyone was looking back and forth at one another and then we saw him. It was the same car with all the dents and bad paint but coming out of the back was a flame ten times the length of the car itself. As it continued in toward town it was gaining speed and not slowing. It didn't take long for us to realize he wasn't going to slow down but was going to continue to increase his speed.

What we didn't know was that in the car he was trying to control the speed with his homemade throttle system which had jammed and he couldn't break it loose. He tried to kill the engine and it wouldn't shut down. As he went past me I could see him fighting the controls when he glanced out the window at me.

He had this goofy look on his face and then he was gone. Five seconds later he went through the front door of the city hall and came out the back wall. When I got to the car I expected to find a dead man in there. Instead I find this guy upside down with his legs sticking through the steering wheel, out cold.

He survived with a broken arm and leg. That solidified Dinky's reputation as a screw off and he never let us down from that day on. I don't know how many crazy things he got himself into, all I know is he spent a lot of time in the hospital. Rumors had it he had bought a bed at the hospital so they would always have room for him. Probably not true.

I realized I had been day dreaming and then looked up at Frank. "You knew all that didn't you?"

"Yes, Dinky's life is no secret to me. As his time came up I began to learn more and more about him. His actions with the dynamite fit his personality perfectly. Yes, he was special in more ways than one.

"Dinky made his choice and he died by it. That's not the fault of Duker's Store. The fact is if Duker's Store knew that the world would be ending tomorrow nothing could be said to anyone about it. That would be held within the store and life would take its course."

It then hit me. "Frank, it's obvious Duker's Store is something special. But that brings about a question that needs to be asked. Is this the only Duker's Store in the world?"

He was listening to me closely. "Yes Delbert that it is. There is no other Duker's

Store anywhere on earth. This is the one and only one."

I expected that. "Then why did it end up here?"

He smiled at me. 'Because this is where granddad wanted it."

"Now wait, I'm not going to accept that answer. This place is something special. There is nothing else like it in this world and yet it was placed here, right here in this spot two hundred thirty-five years ago. Why here? Why this place and not someplace else?"

"Delbert, don't try to dig too deep. It's here because this is where my grandfather decided to put it. That's it and there is nothing else. There was no special process or research done. He walked across this valley and when he got to a certain spot, he took a stake and drove it into the ground and that was the place for Duker's Store.

I don't know why here or where the mystery of Duker's Store came from. All I know is I inherited it and once I decided that I had lived it long enough it was time to let someone else inherit it and that someone is you.

"Over the years you will meet others who will be like Dinky, the many others who have come through that door, each one with their own special story and time. Now let me tell you of another.

Chapter Three

Martha Ann

...It was around the year 1900 when I first knew about Martha Ann Kilpatrick. At the time she was sixteen years old and visiting relatives with her parents here in Brownsville. Martha had been walking around town when she came by Duker's Store. She stopped and looked through the front windows. She then walked over to the door and opened it and stepped in.

Naturally I was there at the door to meet her. I welcomed her and asked if I could help her. She was about five feet four inches tall and weighed about a hundred twenty pounds. She had long auburn hair that reached midway down her back. She had vivid blue eyes and a small nose. She had on a pale blue sundress.

At first she was a little shy and didn't really know what it was she wanted. So I started to walk her through the store showing her all the products we had and trying to give her an idea as to what it was she came in the store for.

I had had others come in just as she had and they too were confused and at a loss as to what they wanted. As we talked, I could tell she was a lonely girl who spent a lot of her time off on her own just as she was here walking through town on her own. Finally, I walked her up to the front counter and there on the counter was a diary. She saw it immediately and was drawn to it.

"Martha, do you like that diary?"

She looked at me and nodded her head.

"Do you know what a diary is for?"

She nodded again as she picked the diary up and started to turn the pages.

"Martha, is that what you're looking for?"

She stopped paging through the diary and then set it back down on the counter. She stood there looking at it and then back at me. "I probably can't afford it?"

"Martha, how much do you have?"

She opened her purse and looked through whatever she carried in it. "I have two dollars fifty cents and that's all."

"Well what do you know that particular diary cost a dollar, do you want to buy it?"

She again looked at the diary and opened her purse, took the money out and laid it on the counter top. "Yes please, I love it and I've always wanted to keep a diary. But I'm not sure what I should write in it."

I picked the money up off the counter and then picked up the diary and walked her over to a couple of chairs by the front window. "Martha, sit down and I'll see if I can explain to you what a diary is for."

She sat there looking at me as I explained to her the purpose of a diary and how personal it was to be. That no one else had any right to look into or read her diary, it was just for her and no one else. All her private experiences and wishes could be entered in the diary and she would have them saved for the rest of her life.

I handed it to her and then reached into my pocket and took out a pen and handed that to her. "Here you can have this and as long as you write in this diary every day that pen will never run out of ink."

"Really, no you're kidding me."

"Martha, I promise you as long as you write in your diary every day that pen will always have ink. The first day you fail to write in your diary the pen will stop working. Furthermore you will never write an entry into a diary of any kind again."

She sat there holding the diary in one hand and the pen in the other. "I promise you I will write in my diary every day for as long as I live."

I smiled at her and she stood up and turned toward the door. I followed her and opened the door for her as she left. Just outside the door she turned to me. "You know me don't you?"

I nodded to her. "Yes Martha Ann I know you well and I wish you a wonderful life."

Several hours later Martha was sitting on the porch swing at her relatives when she opened her new diary for the first time. She sat there looking at it and then took the pen and wrote the day of the week and the date of the month and year at the header of the first page. After doing that she sat there looking at the diary when something odd happened.

She started to see writing on the page where none had been before. Something told her to write what she was seeing in her own hand writing. But first she felt she wanted to start a little differently. So she started to write. "Hi Diary this is my first time writing in a diary and I'm not too sure just what I should write about or how much I should write."

She stopped and sat there looking at the words appearing below what she had just written. She then took the pen and started to copy the words. "It's a beautiful day today. Right now, the sun is at three O'clock and it's warm. This will be our last day in Brownsville. Mom and Dad need to get back to Danbury tomorrow and the day after I need to go back to school.

"My school is a special place for me and I love the teachers and my class mates. So I will be happy to return to class at the first of next week. I have only one problem with that and it's Steve Marshall. He has been being mean to me for the past few months and it makes it hard for me to go to school. I know as soon as he sees me, he will start to tease me and, in some cases, push me around.

"I've reported him to my teacher but that has only made things that much worse. Now he will go out of his way to find me on the weekends and pick on me. I don't know why he is doing this to me. I don't recall my doing anything to him that would warrant this kind of treatment."

She stopped writing down or copying the words when the thought entered her mind. What would I want done to make him stop picking on me? She sat there looking at the diary when the words started to appear again. "If he doesn't stop picking on me I want him hurt and hurt bad. The next time he pushes me I want him to be hurt so bad he has to go to the hospital."

She sat there and then slowly closed the diary and got up and went inside.

The next morning she and her parents got in their carriage and started for home. Her mother and father were in the front seat and she was in the back. It would be a four hour trip back to Danbury, with a one hour stop over at a watering and feed spot along the way.

Martha took her diary out and opened it to the second page. She entered the usual headings and then sat there waiting. Nothing appeared so she took pen and started to write. "Again it's a wonderful day. We are on our way back to Danbury after a time in Brownsville visiting family. Mom and Dad have so much fun during these trips. There is really nothing there for me because I'm the only kid. I wish my aunt and uncle could have a child, that would be fun.

"The horses seem to be a little tired today and are not willing to move too fast. It is warm and getting warmer so I guess dad is not pushing them too hard. In a couple of hours, we will stop so they can be rested up before we finish the trip home. I just love riding through this part of the country. The roads are flat and smooth making the ride a lot more pleasant than other trips we have taken.

"Hope Monday is a better day for me at school. I'm a little worried about Steve. It's been over a week since the last time he picked on me."

Just then words started to appear on the page again and she automatically started to copy them down. "I wonder what kind of injury I would want Steve to receive. Maybe a broken arm and leg, maybe a cut across his face, or a back injury, any one of those would stop him from bothering me. No I think a broken arm would be the right injury. The arm that he hurts me with will be broken between the elbow and wrist."

The rest of the journey home went uneventful, Martha had written in her diary for the second time and that was good. She was building a habit, but it would take a couple of more weeks before it was permanent and customary for her. This day was a Saturday and her parents wanted to be home for Sunday church service. That meant she had a day and a half before she had to face Steve again.

The next morning the family was up early and readied to attend church. Martha told her mom she wasn't feeling very good and she wanted to stay home from church. Her mother checked her for a fever and found none. Martha had always been an early riser and never missed church so her mother accepted the fact that Martha was not well and permitted her to remain home.

After her parents had left for church Martha returned to her bedroom and sat down on the bed and opened her diary. This would be her third day of diary entries. "Told mom I wasn't feeling well this morning and got out of going to church. Maybe I shouldn't have done that but I wanted to make sure I made my daily entry in my diary.

"It's a nice day though it's only eight in the morning. The skies are clear for as far as you can see so it should be nice all day. I heard dad talking to mom this morning. He had an appointment with a business man in the morning to talk over a contract that he wanted to win with that company. I think he should win it and it pays him really good. Don't know what it is all about but I know he wants it bad.

"I'm sure Steve will be waiting for me in the morning as I walk to school. He usually starts to follow me when I pass his house and by the time we get to school he's hit me two or three time. I dread walking by his house. I wish it were someplace else so I didn't have to have Steve following me anymore."

The day passed as usual for a Sunday and that evening while at the dinner table Martha's mother asked. "Martha, do you have your homework done for school tomorrow?"

Martha looked over at her mother. "Yes mom I finished that before we went to Brownsville."

"Good, by the way we will be going to a church prayer session tomorrow evening, we expect you to accompany your father and I."

Great, a prayer session, those are as much fun as having a tooth pulled. She knew she had to go and settled back accepting the fact that when her mother said she was going to do something she did it. Some day she would be grown and of an age when she could make up her own mind as to what she wants to do and where she wants to go. That's only two years away and she felt she could make the wait.

That night as she readied for bed she couldn't get the thought of Steve out of her mind. She decided she would wear one of her older dresses so if he knocked her down it wouldn't be that bad with the old dress. She would hate to see one of her new ones damaged.

It wasn't long before she was asleep and then it was bright outside. A new day and she would have to face Steve. She got up and readied for school selecting her oldest dress out of the dozen or so she owned. As she walked into the kitchen for breakfast her mother looked up. "Martha, that's one of your old dresses go back and put a nicer one on."

Martha looked at her mom. "Mom we are going to be doing some craft things in school today and I don't want to wear one of my good dresses. It might get damaged while were doing the crafts."

Her mother smiled and nodded her head. "Yes, I agree and I'm proud you considered that this morning before leaving for school. Martha, I do believe you're growing up."

Martha ate her breakfast, got her books and placed them on the counter by the back door. She returned to her room where she took out her diary and opened to the next day and started to write. "I'll be leaving for school in fifteen minutes. I know that I'm going to have a hard time today, but it's only for a few minutes going to and coming from school. Steve will do his thing and try his best to hurt my feelings and maybe damage my dress. I can take it."

She put the diary away and left her room. On the way out the door she got her books and her mother gave her a hug and Martha set off for school. She was determined not to let Steve intimidate her, so she took the direct route to school right past his house.

As she turned the corner on his street there he was leaning against the fence in front of his house. As she walked by he smiled at her, you know one of those sly I'm going to have fun type of smiles.

Martha kept walking and Steve fell in behind her not saying a word. After they reached the end of the block and turned the corner and were out of sight of his house he started in. "Get your homework done Martha?"

She said nothing in response.

"Martha I asked you if you got your homework done?"

She kept walking and then looked back at him. "Yes I did thank you."

"Will you let me copy it?"

"No I won't let you copy it. You're supposed to do it yourself."

"Yeah Martha, I know that but I want to copy it and I want to copy it from your papers."

Martha had had it and she stopped and turned toward him. "Steve you cannot copy my homework. That is wrong and you know it. Now please leave me alone and go pick on someone else."

He stood there looking at her and started to laugh. By this time several other kids had been walking by and noticed the exchange going on between Martha and Steve. They knew that Steve had a thing about Martha and so they stopped to watch.

Steve was shaking his head by this time. "Martha, I don't want to leave you alone. You're the only fun I have all day and I miss it when I can't play with you. Besides you wouldn't know what to do if I never bothered you. I think you love it."

Right then he pulled his right arm back and shot a punch out at Martha hitting her in the face and knocking her to the ground. Several of the boys standing by yelled at Steve and started to move toward him. He pointed at them. "This is none of your business so stay out of it or else I'll work you all over next."

He turned back to Martha and reached down and pulled her up. "Now it's your homework or another punch."

She looked him straight in the eyes. "No I will not give you my homework."

The second punch came at her in the same way only this time while it was still half way away from her face the arm broke right in the middle between the wrist and the elbow. It just snapped and dangled straight down toward the ground.

Steve stood there looking at his arm in disbelief and then the pain hit him. He screamed out as it surged through his body and hit his mind. "You broke my arm."

The other kids standing around were just as shocked as Martha and Steve were. Finally one of the other girls yelled. "She didn't even touch you."

Another called out. "You deserve it."

Martha was standing there looking at his arm and then remembering her entry into the diary. She had written that she wanted his arm broken and in that exact spot. She stood there thinking it over and then recalled her entry about not wanting Steve's house where it was. Just then there was a huge explosion and everyone turned in the direction of the sound and there flying into the air was Steve's house. It was in a few thousand pieces but it was his house alright.

Martha turned and walked off toward the school her nose still bleeding from the first punch Steve had taken at her. Her blood was dripping down onto the front of her dress but she continued to walk and not pay any attention to it. As she approached the front door of the school a number of teachers were standing outside watching the remains of someone house floating down around the neighborhood it had once been a part of.

One of the teachers happened to look at Martha as she approached and saw the stream of blood running down her face and onto her dress. She ran over to her. "Martha you've been hurt." At the same time she pulled a handkerchief out of her pocket and started to dab the blood from her face and below her nose. "Martha you've been hurt. Come with me and we'll take care of this."

She never saw Steve again that day. The next time she saw him he had a cast on his arm and was with his parents as they rode their wagon out of town with what was left of their belonging piled high.

Martha had returned home that evening and after being questioned by her mother about her nose and the blood on her dress her mother asked. "Did you see what happened to Steve's house? It was blown to pieces. Is that how you got hurt, a piece of that house hit you?"

As soon as her mother said that Martha grabbed on to it and agreed it was a piece of the exploding house that had hit her. No one else got hit but she did and it hurt. Her mother put her arms around her. "Are you all right honey?"

Martha looked up at her and nodded. "I just want to go lay down for a while, is that all right?"

"Of course it is. Now let's take that dress off and I'll get it cleaned up like new. You lie down and take a nap and I'll come and get you for dinner."

Martha agreed and took her dress off and went to her bedroom and sat down on the bed and took her diary out and opened it to the proper page. "Today Steve had his arm broken while he was hitting me and shortly after that his house was blown into a thousand pieces. Fortunately no one was killed.

"I know you did this diary, but I don't know how. That's all right I'll continue to write in you for as long as I live and I know you will take care of me and all my needs."

She closed the diary and settled back for a nap. She knew in her mind and heart she had something special in the diary. Now all she had to do was determine just what it was she was going to do with it.

That evening, while preparing to go to bed, Martha started to think about the diary and all that had happened that day. The things she had written in the diary about Steve and his house all came true. She knew it wasn't an accident that what she had wanted she had entered in the book and then it happened. She also knew she would have to be careful as to what she wrote. If it was fact, anything she wrote came true then she needed to take care so no one was unduly hurt.

Just before crawling into bed she thought of the teacher who had helped her and shown such a tender concern for her. That was Miss. Burton and she decided she would make an entry into her diary for something nice to be given to Miss. Burton tomorrow.

The next morning at the breakfast table her father was there. He normally was gone before she got up but today he was there and he was happy. He looked at her. "Martha you know that business contract I have been working on? Well I won it yesterday and it's going to pay off well for us. In fact your desire to attend college can now be planned, how about that?"

Martha smiled. There it was the fulfillment of her wish for her father's success in that business venture. Now she was certain whatever she wrote in the diary would come true and that meant she could have and do anything she ever wanted. Still, she knew care had to be taken so no harm would come to anyone due to something she had written into the diary.

What she didn't know or consider was the chain of events that could or would be tied to each event she addressed. Events in life are not just single isolated events. When something happens to one person it will reach out and impact the lives of all those that come in contact with or have an interest with that person. Martha was about to discover that in spades.

It was three weeks later and she had been making entries in her diary on a daily basis. It had become a habit and at the end of each day before going to bed she would sit down and write in her diary. In that three weeks she had asked for nothing, just entering the day's activities as she experienced them.

That evening as she finished her homework she took out her diary and started to write. She had learned Miss. Burton was leaving the school. She had received a letter from a large private school the day after helping Martha and she took the opportunity to fill out the application.

The private school had accepted her and offered her three times her current wages to move to that school. She had accepted and had notified the school principle of her coming departure in three weeks' time.

Martha was sure Miss Burton's good fortune was the result of her entry in the diary. She had considered taking the entry back and then thought about it. She learned when Miss. Burton leaves two other teachers will receive promotions and they will be able to deal with a number of personal needs.

Martha was beginning to understand the chain reaction effect of her diary entries. She now realized she needed to take care before making the entries to try and ensure that even in the chain reaction effect it was what she wanted.

That's how it started. Over the next four years Martha would finish high school and then move on to college. During that time she made entries into her diary every day never missing a single day and always having all the ink she needed from her pen during that time. Martha was now entering her second year of college when she met Phillip.

Phillip Easterling was in his junior year at the same college Martha was attending. They met during a class on Civic Growth in the United States. This particular class was exceptionally boring and by the fourth class session better than half the students had stopped attending class.

Martha was dedicated to all her studies and each class had a particularly specific purpose for her. As a result she attended each session, always the first to arrive and last to leave. It was during this class, the fifth session, when Phillip had entered the room and walked over and sat down beside her. He looked at her. "Do you mind if I sit here?"

She had noticed him several times that semester and had developed a private interest in him. "No I don't mind."

"My name is Phillip Easterling, what is yours?" He asked as he offered his hand.

She took his hand. "My name is Martha Ann Kilpatrick."

He sat there a minute. "Kilpatrick, is that the Kilpatrick's from Danbury?"

She was a little startled by his remark but recovered fast. "Why yes it is. My mother and father live there. I was an only child."

"Well Martha, I'm happy to meet you. Are you doing anything after this class?"

Now she was getting a little giddy. "Well no, I usually go home and do my homework so I can get it out of the way and relax a little."

"How would you like to join me at the parlor for an ice cream, my treat?"

No, she was telling herself you can't get involved with someone at this time. It could mess everything up and besides you don't know this person. "I don't think so. I have several things schedule for this afternoon and this evening, it just wouldn't work out."

He sat there looking at her. "Well maybe some other time then. Maybe we could plan a date sometime in the future if that's all right with you?"

Darn, he wasn't going to give up so she nodded her head. "Yes, I think we could do that. When were you thinking would be a good time?"

He looked at her and smiled. "How about tomorrow night, say around six O'clock?"

Right then the professor started his lecture for the day and she shifted her attention to him. After the class was over Martha was picking up her book when Phillip asked. "Well what about it?"

"What about what?'

"Tomorrow night at six O'clock?"

She stopped leaning over her books and looked up at him. "All right six O'clock. Where are we to meet?"

Now he was smiling. "I'll come by your place and pick you up."

Great now he was going to make a big thing out of this, and all the other girls in the dorm will know about my boyfriend, even though he's not my boyfriend, and the teasing will start. "All right you can pick me up at the dorm."

She returned to her dorm and went directly to her room. When she got there her roommate was out. She sat down at the desk and took her diary out and started to write. "Dear diary I met a boy today. I tried to play hard to get but I've seen him many times and have wanted to meet him and, well you know what.

"Diary, I have to be careful here, there are too many emotions involved between young men and women and this young man is stirring this young woman. Common sense tells me to keep my guard up and protect myself while my emotions are telling me to let it go. Diary, I have been faithful in writing in you every day since I first got you. Now I need your wisdom and common sense to step in and steer me in the right direction.

"I want this young man but not right now. Keep him dedicated to me and soften his desires for me at this time. When the time comes and I'm ready and wanting a relationship with him, give him all the desire and drive to give me total pleasure and love from then on."

She closed the diary. She had never done anything like this before and if the diary granted her wish then Phillip was hers whenever she wanted that special time to start. She sat there looking at the diary and put it back in the desk drawer, got up and moved over to her bed and laid down and fell asleep.

The next day at class Phillip came in and sat down beside her. "Hi Martha, hey about tonight, is it all right with you if we just went to a movie and then called it a night. I've got a terrible day tomorrow and I'll need to turn in early?"

She sat there thanking her diary and then looked at him. "Yes Phillip that will work just fine, whatever you want."

That night turned out to be great and they were home early without a single word said about desires or touching. That night she sat on her bed writing in her diary. "Thank you for working this out for me. I now know you have my best interests ahead of all else. I will love Phillip all his life and we will have a special life together."

She set the diary down and went to sleep.

It must have been around three in the morning when something woke her up. There standing at the foot of her bed was her roommate Jean reading her diary. Martha sat up and reached out to grab the book when Jean pulled it away from her. Martha got out of bed. "Jean I want that diary back right this minute. You have no right messing around with someone else's property, so please return it to me now."

Jean was laughing by this time and still paging through the diary. "You actually believe that anything you put in this book will come true? You have got to be the biggest nut case I have ever seen."

Martha was now stalking Jean and worked her into a corner and then reached out and took the diary from her. Jean looked at her. "I can't wait to tell this to the rest of the dorm. They'll laugh their heads off."

Martha turned and walked over to her bed and sat down looking at Jean. "You can't be serious about telling everyone else about my diary, everything in it is my own personal thoughts and wishes."

"Martha, that thing is the funniest thing I have ever seen. You think you can ask that diary to save Phillip for you until you're ready for him, girl that just plain nuts.

"No, I believe this should be discussed by everyone. You should learn never to leave anything lying around like that. It just invites someone to come along and take advantage of it. In a couple of weeks you'll get over it and life will be as usual except maybe Phillip will be gone."

Jean then walked over and got back in her bed and rolled over. Martha sat there looking at her and then opened the diary, took the pen and started to write. "Jean has discovered our special secret. She is planning on spilling everything to the entire dorm in the morning. I don't think we can let her do that.

"Before she can talk to anyone she must be dealt with in whatever manner possible to ensure she never ever talks about our relationship. Whatever is needed she must not be permitted to say a word to anyone about anything that has to do with this diary."

She then slipped the diary under her pillow and went to sleep. The next morning she got up and placed the diary in the locked drawer of her desk and then went to shower. Jean was still in bed and was probably planning on sleeping late.

When Martha returned to the room Jean was sitting on the edge of her bed looking down at the floor. She had a knife in her right hand and there was a stream of blood coming out of her mouth. There on the floor between her legs was her tongue.

Martha stood there looking at Jean. "Jean what have you done? Jean look at me what have you done?"

Martha opened the room door just as two other students were walking by. "Help me Jean has cut her tongue out."

The two rushed into the room and seeing Jean started to scream. Seconds later others started to show up and had the same reaction. Finally the house mother entered the room and seeing Jean she ran out to get help.

Ten minutes later she returned with a doctor and nurse. They laid Jean down and started to work on her, the knife fell to the floor beside her tongue. Everyone else was sent out of the room.

Jean never returned to the dorm and was sent home to her family. The best that could be learned was she had gone completely insane after cutting her own tongue out. Martha's secret about the diary was still secure.

That event brought about the full realization Martha could control anything or anyone she wanted to and if there was reason she could eliminate the problem with little effort. That was going to lead to a most unbelievable set of circumstances within the next three months.

Slowly the realization of her capabilities started to settle in on Martha. She

75

no longer was thinking like a young woman that cared and gave assistance to whomever needed it. In her place as a woman that was both calculating and controlling, a woman centered on herself and her ability to turn anything to her will and her advantage.

The first indication something serious was going on was when she suddenly became a straight 'A' student. It was noted she had not increased her level of effort but had in fact reduced her efforts.

She was attending only half the classes and was still acing her tests and project assignments. In addition she was becoming more manipulative of others. People who were openly opposing her were having accidents or misfortunes yet nothing pointed to her as the cause or perpetrator of those happenings.

It was toward the end of the school year; Phillip had been running errands for Martha and had just returned to her place. He set the box down on the table and then turned to Martha. "Martha I'm going to have to go home this weekend. Mom called this morning and told me dad was not doing well. They are both quite old and I need to check in on them to ensure there are no other problems."

Martha was setting up some book references and listening to Phillip at the same time. "No I think I'm going to need you this weekend. Your parents can wait till next weekend, besides they're never going to be able to completely care for themselves."

The cruelty of her comment hit Phillip hard. He turned to her anger flashing in his eyes. "Damn you Martha my parents are the most important people in the world to me and when mom calls I go and I don't care what you think."

Martha turned to him. "Phillip I need you here and you are going to stay. If you're concerned about your parents then I'll take care of your concern. After tomorrow morning they will never need you again, at their age they're not worth that much anyway."

Phillip instantly went in to a rage and struck Martha across the face. "You little bitch, you think for a minute you can just toss my parents into a garbage heap and think nothing of it. I don't know what's going on here but in the last three months you've gone from a caring and loving person to a self-centered bitch and I'm fed up with you.

"You can live as you want but I'm done with you and all you stand for. You don't need me anyway. You can take care of yourself. I'm going to go home and check in on my parents and then when I get back I'll be completing my studies and graduating and then getting to hell out of here. One thing I know, I will never spend another minute with you."

With that he turned and walked out of Martha's room and headed back to his dorm to pack and leave for home. Martha stood there watching the door waiting for him to come back but he didn't. After an hour she went to her desk and took the diary out and sat down to write.

Her anger was raging through her body and mind as she picked the pen up and started to write. "He must die, but first of all I want his parents to die. In fact I want them to die violently just after he arrives home.

"Then I want him to be arrested for their deaths and he is to be convicted and then sentenced to death. I want his sentence to be carried out within two weeks after he is convicted and sentenced.

"He is to suffer for every word he said to me and every thought he had about me. Of course I'm talking about Phillip. He will leave to go home tomorrow morning and he will arrive and his parents will die a violent death while he is there and then it all will go bad for him."

She closed the diary and sat back. No one talks to her that way and lives. Her mind had made the final jump and now the evil inside of her was in full control. From then on she would be a living nightmare for anyone and everyone she met.

The following morning Phillip left for his parents place. It was a six hour trip on horseback at the time. When he got home he entered the house to find his parents in the living room reading. As they looked up his mother stood up and walked up to him.

Without warning he reached out and grabbed her around the neck and started to choke and shake her violently. He did it so fast he broke her neck and crushed her esophagus at the same time.

His father stood up yelling at him to stop. He dropped the dead body of his mother on the floor and then walked up to his dad and started to slug him in the face and about the head with every ounce of force he could muster. In less than fifteen seconds he was dead on the floor beside his wife.

A neighbor heard the noise and screaming coming from the house and called the police. They arrived within minutes of Phillips' killing his parents. He was in a daze looking at his hands and the blood dripping off of them. The officers took him down, cuffed him and hauled him out of the house and back to the station.

By now the media had gotten word of the event and were showing up at the residence asking questions. The police held an impromptu media briefing. "At three O'clock this afternoon Mr. and Mrs. Bradly Easterling were killed by their son Phillip. Phillip Easterling has been arrested and is currently being booked into the county jail on two counts of murder.

"Evidently Phillip Easterling came home from college after being notified his father was not doing well. When he arrived at the Easterling home he immediately killed both his parents. He killed his mother first by choking her and breaking her neck. After that he beat his father to death with his bare hands. We can give no additional information at this time."

The news hit the wires within an hour after that briefing. Martha heard about the event when one of her friends came over to the dorm and told her of the news release. She sat there smiling, knowing she owned the world.

Two days later she was at the jail where Phillip was being held. She had been granted visitation rights. That was the day after she had made the entry in the diary, she wanted to see Phillip.

When he entered the room he walked over to the table and sat down on the other side from her. They sat there looking at one another. Finally she sat forward. "That's for telling me you were done with me. That's for putting your parent before me. You will never do that again.

"If you want to live, I can get you out of this but you must commit yourself to me and understand any false move on your part will result in your immediate death. Now do you want out of this mess?"

Phillip sat there as the realization hit him this creature was the one who had set this thing up. He didn't know how she did it but he was sure she did do it and she could kill him as well. Finally he sat back. "All right if you get me out of this I will pledge myself to you. I don't want it to end this way I just want to get out of here and live a quiet life."

"All right I'll leave you for now and you should be out in a day or two."

Martha left Phillip in the meeting room and went to a local hotel and took a room. That evening she sat down with her diary and set things up for the next day. "Phillip has learned his lesson and will never be a problem for me again. Make arrangements for him to be released, no longer a suspect in his parent's deaths."

Two days later Phillip was standing on the steps of the court house when the detectives who arrested him walked up. "We no longer have any evidence that you committed those acts against your parents. We are sure someone else was involved. By the way here is a note from Miss. Martha Ann."

Phillip read the note and then walked over to the hotel and up to the third floor to room 318. He knocked on the door and she opened it a few seconds later. Phillip stood there looking at her, now what?"

She smiled at him and opened the door all the way. "Come in Phillip, let's talk."

He walked into the room and she followed him. After she had closed the door he turned to her. "I should kill you right here right now."

"I knew you would say that and so I've taken steps that will ensure you do nothing stupid. Phillip you don't know it but you are about to start a life that will be both wonderful and highly profitable. The life you will live will be one of great wealth.

"Now it's time for you to get over this issue and move back into the position you had with me before. Phillip, whether you think so or not I love you and you mean everything to me. I have made arrangements for you ever since we met and I still will from now on."

He stood up looking at her. "You love me? Bull shit, you don't know what love is. You think if you give me anything and everything, I will be happy. Martha only a bird in a cage being fed daily is happy. I'm not a bird.

"You've gone to a lot of trouble to try and bring me back under your control. Well it won't work. My hate for you is deep and unchangeable. You have only one choice in regards to me and that is to kill me. If you don't I will in time kill you. You can't watch your back every day, every hour or every minute. The day will come when there is an opening and on that day I will kill you.

"So I would suggest you take the first step and finish me off now, because if you don't no matter where you go or what you do I will follow and one day I will take my revenge." He then turned walked over to the door, turned and looked at her and shook his head, opened the door and left.

She picked up her diary and started to read. "If he rejects me and leaves this room he is to die within the hour."

She reached down to pick up the pen and it wasn't there. She started to search for it but couldn't find it anywhere. She had to find her pen and she had to find it before midnight or else the diary would no longer work. Worse yet if she didn't find her pen and write in the diary before midnight she would die.

She had lived for one hundred and ten years writing in her diary every day without failure and now the pen was gone. She had attended over two dozen colleges and it was while she was at this college, she met Phillip and fell in love for the first time.

Her powers over those around her had held strong for all these years yet when she met love for the first time she fell in more ways than just her feelings. She fell to the point where she became careless and destroyed both Phillip and herself.

Phillip, it had to have been Phillip, he took the pen when he left the room. He knew she needed that pen to write in her diary and he took it. She had to find him. She ran out of the room and down to the lobby of the hotel. She ran out the front door and there in the middle of the street was Phillip with a group of people standing around him.

He was lying on the street having been run over by a trolley car just moments before. There beside him were the remains of a crushed pen. She kneeled beside him and picked the pen up and held it there looking first at him and then at the pen.

The woman across from Martha was watching her when Martha said. "Phillip how could you do this. How could you leave me this way?"

Martha stood up and walked back to the hotel and up to her room. She sat down at the desk and laid the pen down beside the diary. She didn't move the rest of the evening and as the clock reached midnight and started to chime she started to change. By the time the twelfth chime ended her head dropped onto the desk top.

The next morning the cleaning woman opened room 318 and found a very old lady sitting at the desk with her head on the desk, she was dead. All that was there on the desk beside her was a broken pen...

Frank sat there looking at me. Delbert, many lives have passed through this place, some bad and some good. What they come here for are their own desires. It is our place and purpose to fulfill those desires. Martha wanted a diary and so we had one here for her. The pen was a gift for a rather bashful and beautiful young girl. What she did with them was her decision.

Chapter Four

Earnest Richmond

"Frank, do all purchases that people make end in a bad way?"

"Delbert, you would be surprised to know that it's about fifty-fifty. This store is not here to create trouble or problems for those who shop here. This store is here to provide whatever it is those people need or are looking for.

"Let me tell you about another man that came here one day. His name was Earnest Richmond, he didn't live in this area, he was just passing through, but something brought him to stop and come into the store. When he did he found an item that he wanted, or maybe actually needed."

...Earnest Richmond was a single man with a successful career and everything and anything he wanted. He had no lady friends and in fact had no friends at all. He did have a dog and that I guess you would have to say was his only and best friend in the world.

Ernest was fifty-seven years old, about six feet six inches tall. He was slender and well built. He appeared to be highly intelligent and carried himself quite well.

At the ripe old age of sixteen he made a technological discovery that resulted in his becoming extremely rich. So, by the time he was thirty-seven and tired of fighting the business game he retired and took his billions and started to travel around the country.

Personality wise he was impossible. Everything he did and thought of was in relationship to what it did for him, regardless of what it did to others. Everything was the bottom line and nothing stood in his way, not even those who did the work or those who did the dirt as well. Generally speaking he was probably the most hated boss on the face of the earth.

It was a cool and overcast day in the middle of October when he drove through town. On that particular day he had no real plans other than ending up in Placer City three hundred miles to the south. As he drove down Main Street he came to Duker's Store and pulled into the parking spot.

"Why the hell had he done that?" He thought to himself. He sat there looking at the store. "Damn place is a fire trap. Must be at least a hundred year old surely there's no real reason why I need to stop here?"

He sat there for several minutes contemplating whether he should leave or not. I was standing inside the door watching him as he tussled with his reasoning for pulling into the parking spot.

Finally after sitting there for five minutes or so he got out and walked up to the door. He stood there looking at the door and then reached out and opened it. As he entered the store I was standing there to greet him. "Good morning, welcome to Duker's Store."

He walked past me. "You actually make a living in this place?"

"Why, yes I do a rather nice living at that."

He glanced back and continued walking into the store. I followed him as he started to walk down the aisles looking at my products and stopping every so often and picking something up. He then turned to me. "I don't know why the hell I came in here? You don't have anything in this place that even comes close to my wanting to buy it."

I smiled at him. "Well maybe you just need to walk around for a while, maybe you'll find something after all. Besides you're the only one in the store and I have all the time in the world to assist you."

As he walked along he started to talk to himself. "No one could make a living in this place. Hell, I'm the only customer here, he's got more products on his shelves than he could ever hope to sell, and the place is about as dreary as any place I've ever been."

This went on for about a half an hour when he got to the end of one of the aisles and stopped. He was looking up at the wall and there hanging from the wall was a golf club. He looked at me and then back at the club. "How old is that club anyway, it looks like it's a couple of hundred years old."

I looked up at the club. "Oh, no it's almost brand new. The maker just made it look that way. I guess you could say it's a conversation piece."

He kept looking at the club and finally looked at me. "I want to see that club. Get it down for me."

"Of course, let me get my ladder and I'll have it down for you in a jiffy."

He stood there waiting as I went into the back room and got the ladder and then walked back to where he was standing and set up the ladder. At that point he pushed me aside and went up the ladder himself and grabbed the club and started back down.

As he stepped off the ladder he turned to me. He had a different look on his face and he held the club up, looking it over, how much?"

I looked at the club and then him. "Make me an offer?"

"What, what did you say? Make you an offer. This is a store, is that right?"

"Yes sir it is and a rather fine store at that."

He was shaking his head. "You say you make a good living off this place?"

"That's right, I make very good living off this place."

"I don't see how you can when you stand there and ask a customer how much he would pay for an item. That should be marked on the item itself."

"I understand what you're saying but here at Duker's Store we work things a little differently. I asked you what you would pay for the club that does not mean that I will take whatever you offer."

He dropped the club down into the ball address stance and stood there swinging it back and forth. He then took it back up to his face. "It does have a great balance, large head and a good face. You want me to make an offer?"

"That's right I want you to make an offer, but I want you to make the right offer."

Now he was sizing me up and walking back toward the front of the store. "So I'm to guess what the right offer is before you will agree to sell it to me."

"No you are to make an offer and then I will decide if it is the right offer. I'm sure that you will make an offer that I will accept, but you have to make an offer first."

He stopped at the counter, still holding the club in his hand. "I want this club. Don't ask me why but I want this club and I'll pay just about anything for it, how about five hundred?"

I reached out and took the club out of his hand and walked around behind the counter and laid the club on the counter top. He then leaned across the counter. "Stop playing around, I'll give you a thousand for it and not a cent more."

"Earnest you have just bought yourself a new club."

He pulled his wallet out of his pocket and counted out ten one hundred dollar bills and handed them to me. I gave him a receipt and picked the club up and handed it to him. He turned and walked toward the door then stopped and turned back to me. "How did you know my name?"

I smiled at him and walked up to and past him to the door and opened it. "You looked like an Earnest."

He stood there looking at me and then walked up to the door, stopped and looked down at me, without saying a word, and then walked out the door.

I watched as he got in his car and backed out of the parking place and headed down Main Street and out of town, he never came back…

"Then how do you know what happened to him?"

"Delbert I know what happens to everyone that comes in to Duker's Store just as I knew you were coming and that you would be taking over the operation of this store.

"In time you will understand and know what I am saying, but for the time being you will have to wait until it all comes together for you."

"All right what happened to Earnest?"

...Earnest went on to Placer City. The following morning he had a golf date with three associates of his. They all met at the course and Earnest pulled his bag out of the trunk of his car and started walking toward the club house when he remembered his new club. He returned to the car and pulled the club out of the back seat and placed in his bag, replacing his old driver.

The foursome met at the club house and then found a table and sat down waiting for their call to the green. While there they all had a beer and started talking about their last round and he mentioned his new club. "Guys

I was up around Brownsville yesterday and found this old run down store. Let see its name was Dug, no Duker's Store.

"Well, while there I saw this golf club mounted on the wall. At first look it looked like it was really old, I mean like two hundred years old or something. I asked the clerk, one of the strangest people I have ever met, if I could look at the club.

"He walked off and few minutes later he came back with a ladder and then went up and got the club down for me. As I was looking at it I realized that it was not old but a new club made to look old, know what I mean. I asked him how much and he told me to make an offer. So I did. Well after several offers and some bantering I bought the thing and brought it home with me. I've got it with me now and we're going to see how it works.

Everyone was laughing when the call for the Richmond foursome came. As they approached the tee they went through their usual means of determining who would lead out. Earnest came in fourth.

It was a great day, not to hot and no wind. As each man approached the tee and made their shots Earnest stood back being his usual critical self. It was finally his turn and he took the new driver and approached the ball.

Earnest is what you would call a scratch golfer. He does not have a handicap and he usually wins every round he does. As he set up to strike the ball, as he always did, one of the guys said. "Hey Earnest five bucks say you can't hit the green."

Earnest looked at him and started to laugh. You're on buster; get your money out because it's not yours anymore. He took his swing and connected with the ball. As it left the tee you could tell that something was wrong.

First of all it didn't have the velocity that his drives normally have and the damn thing took a hook and landed in the opposing fairway. Earnest stood there looking where the ball went and then looked at the new club.

It had felt great like it had been made for his hand and grip. The swing felt the same and the connection between the face and the ball felt and sounded the same. The only difference was the direction and velocity of the ball. By all his past experience, that ball should have been two thirds of the way down the fairway and dead center.

He paid the guy off and then finished the hole. At the second tee it was his turn again. He looked at the other three. "This time I think I'll put a little more English on it. That first hole was new club blues, so this one should be a lot better."

The same guy leaned toward him. "How about ten dollars this time, same bet."

Earnest hated it when someone acted like they had gotten the best of him and he took the bet. That asshole was going to pay this time or else. Earnest approached the tee and cut one loose. This time the ball literally disappeared. It was way to hell down the fairway when it started to curve and landed between the second and third fairways.

This was getting out of hand. Earnest paid the guy off and then went to find the ball. He found it and was getting ready to address it for his second shot when a thought came across his mind. 'At the next tee be humble. Leave the competition behind and play for the spirit and enjoyment of the game.'

He thought about that as he looked his next shot over. Whatever the thought it was right, he was letting the other guy get to him. He addressed the ball and relaxed and hit a shot to the green. He finished that hole second.

At the third tee the first man had taken his shot and Earnest then set his ball for his tee shot. He approached the ball and was just getting set when the same guy said, "How about fifteen this time?"

Earnest set the head of the club on the ground and turned to the guy. "Know what, I think I'll pass on this one. With the new club and all that I'm just not playing well and I need to concentrate on my game and not a wager. Is that all right with you?"

The other player nodded his head. "Yeah I understand I've been there and besides that it's not fair."

Earnest nodded back. "Thank you."

He then set himself and made his swing. When his club connected with the ball he knew right then and there that it was a great connect. It sounded perfect and he felt good.

Fairway three is four hundred sixty-five yards long and had a dog leg to the left about three hundred eighty-five yards out. The green sat on a small hill at the end of the fairway and was flat across the whole of the green. On this day the hole itself was located at the back right of the green.

As the ball left the head of the club it took off as if shot from a gun. The four of them watched as the ball continued to climb and then started its arch. At the same time it started a gradual curve to the left as it approached the dog leg.

Once it was well into the dog leg it dropped to the ground and bounced three times and then rolled up onto the green, across the green to the right stopping three feet from the hole.

There was absolute silence as he stood there looking where the ball had gone. He then looked at the club and then back down range toward the third green. The betting golfer walked up to him and put his hand on his shoulder. "That was just about the best damn golf shot I have ever seen anyone make. Good game."

The foursome finished the first nine and while taking their break Earnest was adding up his score for the first nine holes. Par was thirty-six and he had a thirty-three at that point. He sat there looking out at the tenth tee and thinking about how he had addressed the ball and swung the club and how perfect it had all felt.

It dawned on him that his good fortunes had started once he had admonished himself and settled down and played the game and left the bantering behind.

Twenty minutes later they were on the tenth tee and he was teeing up first. By now he realized that the more relaxed and less critical he was of himself and the others the better his game. He was accustomed to criticizing everyone and everything and to stop doing that took a lot of concentration on his part.

The back nine were spectacular and he came across the eighteenth green with a mind busting sixty-six. That was six under par and he had never done that before. He was a par shooter and had a number of sub-par rounds, but this was nuts. This was way outside his norm. That new club had paid off for him.

Now Earnest was retired, but from time to time his old company would call him for help. They hardly ever did and for good reasons. When they called the criticism and belittling of everyone he met while there was painful and hurtful. They only called when things had gotten so bad they had to.

This time the call came and he listened to what they were dealing with. He checked his calendar and made a date to be there in three days'.

As he hung up he was livid. "How the hell could they let something like that go this long before calling? Damn I'm going to kick some asses when I get there."

Just then he looked over at his golf bag and the new club sitting in it. 'That kind of activity will do nothing to improve or correct the situation. All it will do is create hard feeling and make the job of correcting the problem that much more difficult.'

He sat there nodding his head. 'Yeah that's right, it would create problems and problems he did not need.'

Three days later he was at the business sitting in on a meeting addressing the difficulty they were having. Everyone was on pins and needles waiting for the inevitable explosion that had to come.

Finally the owner finished his presentation to Earnest and sat there waiting for all hell to bust loose. Earnest was looking over the paperwork and he saw the problem. Hell that same issue had caught him several times and he sweated blood trying to deal with it.

The solution was rather simple when you compare it to the overall complexity of the systems they were working with. He stood up and walked around to the head of the table and then turned toward the writing board and picked up a pen.

He started to lay it out on the board while talking. "The problem you are having is an old one. One that I have ran into before and managed to figure out after a few nights of hard work.

"There's no reason to be concerned about it, all it needs is two simple adjustments. I would recommend that you put together a protocol for this process so that when it happens again you won't have to call me and spend a bunch of money."

When he finished, the new owner walked up to him. "Thanks Earnest we've learned a lot here today. Can I take you out to dinner?"

Earnest stood there for a few seconds. "No, but if you have the time I would love to play a round of golf with you."

The owner, Mark Langford stood there looking at Earnest. He had never acted this way before but he sure was now. He had heard about Earnest's golf game and felt he really didn't want to be on the receiving end of one of those situations. None-the-less he felt he owed something for the job Earnest had done and agreed to a round of golf.

Two hours later they were on the course and just starting at the first tee. Earnest let Mark go first and then teed his ball. He looked down course and then addressed the ball. What would follow was one of the most astounding events any of the two had seen along with the cadies that were with them.

Earnest's ball left the tee with a loud crack as the head of the club met it. It went into a climb out of the tee area and straight at the green three hundred seventy-four yards away. The arch was perfect and the ball started down, zeroing in on the green.

It landed just short of the green and took two quick and tight hops and then started to roll. The next thing Earnest knew he had made his first hole in one. To Earnest this was amazing in that it was his first hole in one, ever.

After their celebration and completing the first hole they moved over to the second tee. Because Earnest had won the first hole he had tee privileges and stepped forward and mounted his ball on the tee. As he addressed the ball, he looked down range at the green a full three hundred ninety yards away.

For the second time his clubs head met the ball at the precise point that sent it arching toward the green. It sounded like a baseball bat hitting the ball for a home run. They stood there watching as the ball curved down and hit the ground right before the green and started to roll.

The cadies went nuts as the ball rolled across the green and dropped into the hole. Earnest couldn't believe his eyes. Two holes in one in two consecutive holes, that was unheard of.

Mark stood there looking at Earnest and then down range to the green. He walked over to him. "I have a feeling this is going to be the strangest day I have ever witnessed."

They shook hands and headed for the green where Mark finished his hole and then they started walking toward the third hole.

At the tee for the third hole Earnest approached the ball. This hole was four hundred eighty-nine yards and he was sure that he had no chance of a hole in one, let alone reaching the green. He addressed the ball and took his swing.

It was the same as the other two drives at holes one and two. This one landed about fifty yards short of the green and rolled another fifteen yards before coming to a stop. That was a four hundred fifty-four-yard shot, something he had never done before. He chipped to the green and then one putted for an Eagle. In the first three holes he had shot two Holes in ones and an Eagle.

He stood there with Mark as they waited for the fourth tee to open up. By this time the word was getting around that someone was playing the game of their life. It was about then when people started to show up and a gallery was forming for the twosome.

A week ago Earnest would have gone stomping off the course mad as hell that so many people were bothering him. But he had changed and he knew it. Something was going on within him that he never thought would happen. He was enjoying himself and it was not just that, but others were sharing that enjoyment with him.

A young boy walked up to him. "Mister, would you sign my golf ball?"

Earnest looked down at the kid and while looking at him saw himself in those eyes. He looked over at his father and motioned him over to him. As the father walked up to Earnest he asked. "Has your son been playing golf very long?"

The father looked at the boy and put his hand on his shoulder. "I started teaching him when he was five years old, he's fourteen now."

Earnest looked at the boy. "How are his school grades?"

The father again looked at his son. "His mother and I agreed that as long as he kept his grades at a 'B' average or better we would let him pursue his interest in the game."

"And how are his grades going?"

"I'm proud to say he is holding an 'A' average at this time."

Earnest looked around and motioned for the father and son to follow him over under some trees. "Mister I don't know why I'm doing this but when I looked your boy in the eyes something told me that I needed to do this and do it now.

"Where does your son want to go to college?"

The father looked down at the ground. "We haven't talked about that. I don't think we're going to be able to afford that for him."

That remark hit Earnest hard and he stepped back leaning against the tree. He looked at the man and then the boy and at that point signed the golf ball the boy had given him. He then asked. "Son if you could go to college where would you want to go?"

The boy looked at his dad and his dad nodded toward Earnest. "Sir I would want to go to Cornell and if I did well then MIT."

That caused Earnest to stand back up and look at his father again. "You have high plans young man."

He knew what he was going to do and this time he felt good about it. "I'll tell you what; if you and your father will stay in contact with me on a monthly basis. I want to see that you keep your grades at the same level as they are now.

"When you graduate from high school and if your grades at that time are in the Upper 'B' to upper 'A' level I will cover all your costs to attend Cornell University and if you score well there, on to MIT. How does that sound to you?"

The boy's father almost passed out. He grabbed his son and stood there looking at Earnest. "Sir I hope you're not playing a game with us. But if you're serious I think my son would do anything to make it to those schools."

The boy just stood there and then after his father finished he started to nod his head. "You really mean that mister?"

Earnest looked off toward the crowd and then back to the boy. "First of all my name is Earnest Richmond. Does that name mean anything to you?"

The boy started to nod his head. "Yes sir you're one of the richest men in the world."

"Well I don't know about that but I have enough money where I can afford to cover your schooling. Besides that I like you and I think you're special."

He then looked at the father and pulled out his wallet and opened it up. He found and pulled a small white card out of the wallet and handed it to the father. "Sir what is your name?"

"Mr. Richmond my name is Thomas Stillard, this is my son Steven."

"Mr. Stillard, that card I just gave you is a direct line to me and my office. I am going to call that office right now and advise my staff that you are a priority interest of mine and that Steven here is to be given top priority at all times.

"Please, starting next month I want you sir to call my office and give my staff a report on your sons schooling and activities. Now one condition of this project is that Steven continues to play golf. Is that agreed?"

Thomas was standing there with tears running down his face. "Mr. Richmond I'm not sure just what I should say. I'm stunned by this and I know that my wife, Steven's mother, will feel the same. Yes sir I will do that."

"There was one other thing I want you to do Thomas."

"Yes sir what's that?"

"Thomas you are to talk to no one about this. This is private between your family and me is that understood?"

Thomas was nodding his head, "Whatever you say sir."

"Thank you Thomas, now I need to get back to my game."

Earnest returned to his game and continued on. The fourteenth tee was spectacular as well. By the end of the day he had the course record nailed down and was in the running for the lowest 18 hole score ever played.

That evening, back at his hotel, he set his bag of clubs down and pulled out the new Duker's Store club. He stood there looking at the club and thinking about what had happened to him since he bought that club.

The first thing that stood out was when he was his usual obnoxious self his game was terrible. Second when he was agreeable and treated people the way they should be treated his game was beyond his wildest dreams.

Third when he did that special thing for Steven his game was beyond any measurable degree of improvement. He even made the pros look bad.

He walked back and forth looking at that club. He had spent a thousand dollars for it and he wouldn't take twenty thousand now. There was something about that club that changed him, and to the good. As he continued to think about his experience, the Stillard boy kept coming back into his mind. What was it, what was eating at him?

The next morning Earnest got up and decided to go down to the company and talk to Mark about yesterday. He called and made sure he was available and then set out for the company.

On his way out the door he grabbed his Duker's Store club and went down to the main entrance of the hotel. As he approached the front door one of the hotel personnel walked up to him. "Mr. Richmond, do you need a ride?"

"Why yes I do."

"Right this way sir. Our company limo just got back and needs to make a run back to the airport and your company is on the way. Please let us drop you off."

"Thank you I would appreciate that."

He got in the back seat and sat back and the limo headed toward his old company offices. As they pulled into the main parking area the limo stopped at the front door and Earnest got out and started walking toward the door. As he approached he heard a voice behind him. "Sir, Mr. Richmond, you forgot your golf club."

He turned and the young driver came running up to him with club in hand. I thought you may want this being that you brought it out with you."

"Thank you young man, what's your name?"

"Turner sir, Theodor Turner."

Earnest stood there a minute. "Theodor how long have you been driving that limo?"

The boy looked back at the car. "About three years now."

"And has your pay increased an appreciable amount in that time?"

"Other than the cost of living increase no sir."

"Do you want a job that will pay you considerably more than what you're getting at this time?"

The boy was looking at him like he wasn't too sure what he should say let alone be talking to a customer. "Sir, I like this job but if a good one came along that would provide me with a better income, yes sir I would be a fool not to take it."

"All right Theodor, I'm making you a job offer at this time. If you accept I want you to complete the job you have been sent out on and then I want you to go to your boss and give him two weeks' notice, understand?"

He stood there looking at Earnest and then back at the car. "Sir, I hope this doesn't queer the job offer but could you give me an idea as to the pay?"

Earnest smiled and reached out and patted the boy on his shoulder. "Theodor whatever you're receiving right now I'll triple. You will be my direct assistant and you will spend your time driving and traveling with me.

"You will not be a servant. You will be my direct personal assistant in my business and travels. When we go to a hotel it will be a suite with two bedrooms so that you will remain with me at all times. I have a bunch of plans in my head and its more than one man can do on his own.

"Now, how about it?"

Theodor stood there looking at this man he knew nothing about and then he knew he had to go for it. "Sir I accept your job offer and I promise you I will give you everything I have."

Earnest again smiled at him. "Theodor I can assure you that you will earn every cent you receive. But at the same time, you will enjoy every minute of it. Now go make that run for the hotel and then go see your boss.

I'll come back later and have a talk with the hotel manager."

Theodor nodded and turned and started toward the car. He stopped half way there and turned back to Earnest. "Thank you, I don't know what I'm getting myself into, but I do know that it's the right thing to do."

With that Theodor was off and Earnest turned and walked into the office carrying his golf club with him. As he walked through the door Mark Langford was just walking up to the door. "Hey now that's the way to be treated." As he looked past Earnest as the limo was pulling away.

"Yeah, the hotel had it going to the airport so they gave me a ride. I liked the young man driving so I just hired him as my personal assistant."

"Now why would you do something like that?"

Earnest looked at Mark. "Because when you and I are finished here today you'll understand and may consider hiring one yourself.

"Now Mark, let's find a place where we can sit down without being disturbed for two to three hours. I have some ideas that I think you're going to be interested in and if everything goes right you, my friend, are going to become extremely wealthy."

As they walked down the hall Earnest was swinging the club in cadence with his walk. Once they found a quiet place Mark sat down and looked at Earnest. "All right how are you going to make me rich?"

Three hours later they came out of the room and Mark had a smile on his face and a new bounce in his walk. "You're sure this will work?"

"Mark, my friend, not only will it work but it will work so well we will have people knocking down the door wanting to be involved.

"I need to get back to my hotel, would you call me a cab?"

Just as Earnest said that he heard a familiar voice, "Hi Mr. Richmond I, have the limo out front waiting for you."

"Theodor what are you doing here I thought you went back to the hotel?"

"I did but my boss called me in and said he had a message that you needed a ride back and he sent me."

Earnest stood there looking at Theodor and then at Mark. "Mark did you have someone call for the limo for me?"

"No, you and I have been in a meeting all this time and I've talked to no one."

Earnest was puzzled by this happening. How would anyone know he needed the ride and then call for the limo from the hotel to pick him up? He was standing there with the shaft of the club resting on his shoulder when he heard it. "I knew you needed a ride so I got one for you."

He looked at the other two and then realized the voice was coming from the club. No, clubs don't talk it was something else, but what?"

"Earnest, this is the first time I have been able to really connect with you. You heard me right the first time. As long as you continue to progress in your current growth I will be here to aid you.

"You're doing well and you'll succeed in anything you attempt as long as you keep growing and continue to be the new Earnest that you are today. I will discuss this situation with you later on while we're alone, so stay with it for now and you'll understand everything later on."

He held the club up looking at it and then he looked at Mark and laughed, "Hell it must have been the club."

All three of them started to laugh. Earnest turned and started walking down the hall toward the entrance and the limo waiting for him. A whole new life was opening up to him and he was beginning to like it…

"Delbert, I can assure you that Earnest did well and became even wealthier than he had been before. Mark Langford went on to become a major influence in the corporate world as well as becoming quite wealthy in his own right.

"As for Theodor, well he worked for Earnest for five years, eventually going out on his own and becoming a leading business financier himself. Today he is a force unto himself.

Steven Stillard made it to Cornell University and eventually graduated from MIT and is today a leading scientist in the field of automation.

"You see, not all things purchased from Duker's Store results in bad things happening to the person making the purchase. In this case a number of people were touched and helped with the purchase of that club.

"Now you may ask if the club actually did talk to Earnest. The answer to that is yes and no, the club did talk to him but it was all within Earnest himself. As he developed he became aware of his own inner talents and one of those was the ability of his mind to reach out and do things such as making phone calls or touching people needing help.

"To this day he is still doing for others through the process of his minds ability to do things without his having to physically be there.

"The club, he never lets it out of his sight. No one dares touch that club or move it unless they want to be taught another lesson. And when or if someone moves his club he responds.

"How does he do it?"

"Well he can't be the Earnest he once was, so he gets up and walks over to wherever that person moved the club and picks it up and then turns to the person and smiles at them. He then simply tells them that the club never ever leaves his side. Enough said."

When Earnest no longer needs his club, probably the day he dies, the club will return to its rightful place there on the wall.

Chapter Five

Luke Mann

Delbert, I guess what I'm trying to relate to you is that this store is beyond this time and those who live here in Brownsville. As I tell you of these people you will see that time is of little importance. What is important are the people and what they did with their lives after their visit to Duker's Store.

It is important that you open your mind and listen to what I am telling you. Once you walked through that door the Store had determined you were the next owner, that's why you cannot walk or run from it. I would suggest you open your heart and mind and learn from what I am telling you.

I know it's hard and that you still insist that you're not going to remain here or own this store, but I can assure you, you will.

Now for the next person in our tour of Duker's Store. His name is Luke Mann. This time, when Luke walks through that door, he was on a mission, a mission that Duker's can never let him carry out.

...I met Luke in 1998 just three weeks before Christmas. The day was a Tuesday. It had been raining all night and seemed to increase in intensity when the sun came up.

I felt him coming at about nine forty-five that morning and headed for the door to be there when he came through the door. As I walked up to the door I saw a green pickup truck pull into the parking place.

I watched as the man got out of the truck, looked around Main Street, up into the sky and then turned and started walking toward the door. He had a heavy coat on and was wearing a wide brim hat.

As he came through the door I stepped toward him and offered my hand. "Good morning, welcome to Duker's Store."

He stopped short and looked down at my hand and then at me. He reached out with his right hand and pushed me aside as he walked on into the store. "This your store?"

"Yes it is. What can I do to help you?"

"You the only one working here?"

"Yes, there isn't that much business to hire additional personnel. Besides it is only meant to be a one man business."

"Do you sell guns here?"

"I sell anything you want no matter what it is. The question is what do you want?"

He stopped and glanced back at me and then continued into the main area of the store. I want an automatic assault rifle, you have those?"

"If that's what you need I have it? Is that what you need?"

"Can you get me more than one?"

"I can get you any number you want, but you have to tell me exactly what it is you want and how many."

Finally he turned to me. "I don't see a single gun in this place. How the hell you going to be able to sell me the gun I want if you don't have it?"

"Oh don't worry about that. When you tell me exactly what it is you want that item will be here ready for you. Now what do you want?"

121

He stood there a few seconds and then walked up to me and grabbed me by the shirt, right at my neck. "Don't play games with me little man, I'll tell you what I want when I'm ready, understand?"

I was standing on my toes looking him square on the end of his nose. "Sir, you don't have to get physical. I told you I could supply you with whatever it is you want, but first you have to tell be what it is you want."

He let me down and then walked over to the counter. He leaned against it and motioned me over by him. As I approached the counter, he turned facing me with his left elbow on the counter. "All right I'll tell you what I want, but if you don't have it I'll be extremely unhappy.

"Now I'm going to ask for a specific weapon and you had better make good. I want a Glock G41 Gen 4 .45 Auto caliber with two thirteen round clips."

I was watching him. He was nervous and continually looking out the front of the store into the street, as if he was expecting someone to show up at any moment. I smiled at him. "Please sit back and I'll be right back."

As I turned, he reached out and took hold of my right arm. "Now don't you go running out on me, I don't want to have to come looking for you and if I do you'll wish you had been straight with me."

I looked at my arm and then reached over and removed his hand. "I never leave my store and I will never run out on any customer. I must go into my supply room and get the weapon you just asked for. It won't take me long so sit down and I'll be right back."

Five minutes later I was setting a brand new Glock G41 Gen4 weapon on the counter in front of him. He looked down at it and then back at me, "Brand new?"

"Absolutely, it still has its packing grease on it."

"Can I get two boxes of ammo as well?"

I set the two boxes on the counter beside the gun. "There you have it, now is there anything else you want?"

He picked up the gun and was turning it over in his hand. "Do you have a Colt Model LC6920 AR15 rifle with two twenty round magazines?"

Again I nodded. "Is that what you want?"

"Yeah, do you have one?"

"I'll be right back"

Five minutes later I was setting a brand new Colt Model LC6920 in front of him. "There are two magazines that come with this model."

He was looking both weapons over carefully. "How much for the two of them and can I take them with me now?"

I had to smile. Of course he could take them with him. That's what Duker's Store is all about. Whatever you need we have it now. "The two weapons will cost you $2,500, which includes two boxes of ammo for each one."

He was reaching into his pocket and looking at me. "I'll take them both."

At that point I cleared my throat, "There is one problem."

He stopped and looked back at me. "What's that?"

I smiled at him. "You can't kill a human being with either of them."

His mouth dropped open and he got this stern and mean look on his face. "Mister that's what guns are made for, they're made for killing people. If you think you can tell me that I can't use either of those guns on people, well you've got another thing coming."

Right then I needed to remain calm and firm as I stood there. "That is right. I can sell you these guns but they cannot be pointed at or used on any human being. Now believe me when I tell you that.

"If you attempt to point either of those guns at any person, anybody, the gun will automatically point to the floor and there is nothing you will be able to do about it."

He stood up and grabbed the Glock and a box of rounds and dropped the clip out of the Glock and then loaded the clip with thirteen rounds. He then slid the breach back and loaded a round into the chamber.

He looked right at me and brought the gun up and placed it at the end of my nose. "And what the hell are you going to do about it?"

All right, I have to admit that I was a little concerned. After all, I had never looked at a gun from that end before and I sure as hell didn't want to be doing it right then. He was mad as hell and I could see his trigger finger tightening on the trigger.

As it tightened on the trigger the gun started to slide down toward the floor. As hard as he tried he couldn't keep it from pointing to the floor. The faster and harder he pulled on the trigger the faster and harder the gun moved toward the floor.

As he finished pulling the round off the gun was pointing straight down at the floor between his feet. The round went into the floor at that precise location, "What the hell anyway?"

You could feel the shock and confusion in his words as he said them. He brought the gun back up and stood there looking at it. "This gun is no good for anything if you can't shoot someone with it."

Brilliant, of course it's not good for killing or shooting people. That is one of the basic rules in Duker's Store; a weapon of any kind that may or could be used against another human being will not function in that way. He had just learned that the hard way.

"Sir, I would suggest that you not buy a weapon here. I'm sorry we cannot sell any weapon that may be used on another human being. If you still feel you need a weapon to use on another being then I would suggest you go elsewhere."

By now the man was completely confused and defeated. "Sir, what is your name and why do you want these weapons anyway?"

He had put the gun down and slipped off the stool and was walking toward the back of the store. He stopped, facing away from me, and then turned. "My name is Luke Mann and I wanted the weapons so that I could start a rebellion."

I stood there looking at him. He was angry and driven but he was not being rational. "Luke, what are you rebelling against?"

"Those people, the ones that keep costing me more and more of my earnings and savings, just so they can play politics with my life. We need to kill them, every single one of them and then start over new with people who have a desire to serve and not fill their own pockets."

Well, I asked him the question and he gave me the answer. It wasn't that clear, but it was an answer. "Luke, who are these people you're talking about?"

"You know, you know who I'm talking about. The ones that do things in the name of their official capacity then increase our costs to cover their stupid mistakes. You know those council people, commissioners and congressmen, all of them."

"Luke, those people are there because we elected them and put them there. They are only trying to do their job and I really don't think that all of them are corrupt. Surely you don't want to kill any of them. Wouldn't it be better if you help get them voted out of office?"

"That doesn't work; they have too many criminals helping them. Besides, we would end up with just another politician and they're the ones I'm trying to get rid of.

"Don't you see we have to do something and do it now and the only thing these people understand is violence? Power is the only thing they understand and the power of the gun is the highest level of power. Everything is so screwed up now I don't think even a revolution could change it."

"Then why do you want to start one Luke. If what you say is true then starting a revolution will gain you nothing, other than killing a lot of people and many of those would probably be innocent ones at that."

He was clearly frustrated and didn't really know just what to say or what to do next. I noticed a tear running down his cheek as he stood there looking at me. "I just want peace and quiet. I'm sick and tired of all the bad going on and seeing no one who is trying to deal with it. We would all be better off dead."

"Luke I'm going to sell you something that I think you really need and it's not a gun." I walked around behind the counter and picked up a small box and set it on the counter top. "Now this item will take a little getting used to, but if you work at it the item in this box will give you everything you need. Do you understand me?"

By now he was starting to walk toward the counter again. He hadn't noticed that the guns were gone, just that I had placed a small box on the counter. As he walked up to the counter I opened the box and slid it across the counter to him.

He looked up at me and then back down to the box. He leaned over and looked into it and then reached in and pulled out a round metal ball. It was about three inches in diameter and weighed about 9.93 pounds.

He stood there balancing the ball in his hand and then looking at me, "Gold?"

I nodded at him. "Yes, 99.999 pure Gold."

He rolled it around in his hand and then set it on the counter top and rolled it around on top of the counter watching it move and seeing the reflection of the lights in it. "What do you want for it?"

I had him at that time. "I want a thousand dollars for it."

A puzzled look shot across his face. He picked it up and bounced it in his hand several times. "It's got to weigh at least ten pounds. That makes it worth around two hundred thousand dollars today. How can you sell it for a thousand dollars and make a profit?"

I smiled at him. "That's not what I paid for it and I can assure you that at a thousand dollars I will make a fine profit."

He wasn't going to take that answer. "No way, if you have any brains at all you would take this to a bank and cash it in."

"Luke, you don't understand, there is something more important about that ball. First of all, have you ever seen a ball of gold? Second, have you ever seen a ball of gold with a finish on it like that one?

"Look at it, look closely and tell me what you see."

He picked it up and brought it up to his face and looked at the surface of the ball. As he did he started to push it away from him then stopped and pulled it back to him. He then started to smile as he stood there looking into that ball. "I can see people moving around and lots stuff in the air. I can't tell what that stuff is but there's a lot of it.

"Everyone seems to be having a good time and some are throwing more of the stuff into the air." He looked at me. "What does it mean?"

"Luke, that is a special ball and right now you need it more than anyone else on the face of the earth. When you buy it you will then know what it is and what you are seeing. From then on it's all up to you as to what you do. The ball will tell you."

He reached into his pocket and pulled out a wad of cash and dropped it on the counter. "Here take what you want."

I stripped a thousand dollars off the wad and handed it back to him. He took the money and put it back in his pocket and then picked up the box and set the ball into it.

He turned and started walking toward the door and I accompanied him. At the door he stopped and turned to me. "You told me

131

that once I bought this ball I would know what it was for and all about. Well now I know and I think I'm going to have one hell of a great time. Thank you."

I nodded to him and opened the door and watched as he got into his truck and drove off…

"Delbert, that was just the beginning."

"Frank, the beginning, the beginning of what?"

"Delbert let me continue."

…After leaving the store Luke drove the two hundred fifty miles back to his home. When he got there he went into his den and placed the gold ball on his desk in front of him. He then picked up the phone and called his best friend and asked him to come over to his place.

An hour later Luke's friend, Paul Fielding, arrived. Luke met him at the front door. Paul walked in and Luke took his hand and shook it. "Paul thanks for coming on such short notice but I have a problem and I think you're just the person to work it out for me."

Paul looked a little confused at this point. "No problem Luke, what's going on?"

Luke motioned for Paul to follow him and he returned to his den and motioned Paul toward a chair. "Paul, can I get you a drink?"

"Yeah Luke, you know my favorite."

Luke set the drink in front of Paul and then moved around to his chair and sat down. He sat there looking at Paul while he took a sip of his drink. "Paul, I had an experience today the details of which I'll not bore you with. As a result of that experience I have made a decision.

"You know my feeling toward the political scene these past few years?"

Paul nodded his head.

"Well I have been thinking about that a lot lately and I have to admit that a lot of my thoughts have not been too pleasant. Frankly I've been frustrated as hell. Well this morning the answer to my frustration finally came to me. Paul I'm going to run for congress."

Paul damn near fell out of his chair and he did spill half his drink down the front of his shirt. "What the hell did you just say; you're going to run for congress?"

"Yeah Paul, that's what I said, I'm going to run for congress."

Paul stood up and started pacing the floor and looking down at his feet. He had known Luke for many years and always knew him as a person with a deep seated dislike for politics and politicians in particular. Now he was saying he was going to run for congress. He looked over at Luke.

Luke raised his hands. "Just a minute Paul, let me finish before you go off on me. Up till this morning I have had an attitude that I would just a soon shoot those bastards as look at them.

"We all know that can't work. You pull a stunt like that and you're dead. But there is a way to get at them and be just what you want to be, a pain in their asses. That is to run for and win a seat in congress.

"Paul, I want to run for the senate seat for this district and you want to know something, I'll win."

Paul was beside himself not knowing what to say or how to react to Luke's proclamation. He stopped, looked at Luke again, and started to say something then went back to his pacing. Luke was totally enjoying himself over the situation and sat there and let Paul stew in it for a while.

After several minutes Paul walked over and sat down. "Luke, I don't know what to hell to say. Up until this moment you have hated politicians with a passion. At times I was concerned that you would do something foolish like shooting one of them.

"Now you're telling me that you want to run for the senate against a three term incumbent. I don't know, this sounds impossible to me."

Luke knew what Paul was saying and was trying to come up with an answer for him. He reached down into the side drawer of his desk and touched the ball. "Paul, listen to me for a few minutes. Yes, you're absolutely right about my attitude toward politicians and I'll tell you right here and now it remains the same.

"That's important because that is what we are going to run on. We the people have had enough of the politicians. I am going to go into congress and create so much turmoil that I'll become a target myself. I am going to run as an independent and my stand will be the corrupting effects of political parties on the everyday life of the average citizen.

"We are going to home in on the political power mongers and the damage they have done to this nation in the past two hundred fifty or so years. We are going to speak out and challenge the people to vote their hearts and not their pockets, to vote their conscience and not their frustration.

"Paul, I'm telling you that we can and we will beat that old butt head and we'll do it in a landslide victory. I'll make one other promise to the people, if I don't live up to my stated actions I will not run the next time around. If I don't live up to my stated actions I want them to vote me out of office."

They both fell quite for several minutes. Paul was still digesting what Luke had said to him. He wasn't sure he wanted to get involved in this, but had always said that if Luke needed anything from him he would be there.

Luke then picked up a sheet of paper and handed it across the desk to Paul. "Paul, this is a contract between you and me. If you agree to assist me in this project I have to have you sign that contract. Please read it carefully because I mean what I say there."

Paul sat back and read the paper handed to him. He looked at Luke and then continued reading finally putting the paper down and bringing his hands up to his face touching his lower lip. "If you are sincere in what you say there then I can agree to it. But if that paper is just a show then I'll walk off no matter what that paper says and you can go to hell."

Luke started to laugh and picked up the paper and turned it toward him, picked up his pen and signed in the space for his signature. He slid it back across the desk to Paul. "It's all up to you now Paul. You sign that paper and everything's going to hit the fan. A good part of the time we'll be running for our lives, our political lives that is.

"What say you, sign and join me or get up and walk out that door. I need to tell you also that if you leave I will still love you and consider you the best of my friends. Also, if you leave that will not change the outcome of this coming election, I will still win."

Paul took the pen and signed his name and sat back, "Now what?"

"Paul, we go down to the state clerk's office and register for the Office of Senator for this district. We then start to build our election committee and put together a budget.

"Now I want to make this clear. If people donate funds to me they do so without any promises of future favors or service they can expect. There will be no conditions. If they donate it will be for one reason and one reason only, they want me to be their next senator."

So the battle engages, Luke's rebellion was in full force and he would pursue it to the end. True to his words he won the election by a landslide. When he moved to Washington DC he took little with him. He knew he was on the outside because of his independent position but he did find three other senators who ran on and won as independents.

They formed their own forum and set to work to shake up the foundations of government. Luke took the first step by building a communication system between him and his constituents. He informed them of every shady deal he discovered between the politicians, their party, and those they were seeking to sell favors to.

The first newsletter lit off a fairly significant explosion in the middle of the senate. Several party senators stood and accused him of misconduct by releasing information that was deemed to be private and not for public access.

He countered with the fact that they were actions that took place in the middle of a public forum and on government time. And furthermore he would continue reporting to his people the actions and conduct of their elected representatives each and every day.

He made it clear that they could block anything he attempted to do and he would accept that. He would vote for or against any and all legislation based on the impact of that legislation on his people.

As things started to get real hairy the other three independents joined him and as a block of four they stood their ground. On the second month Luke again published his newsletter but this time titled it "The Silver Bullet". When he pulled the trigger on this one it nailed four older senators down on their personal spending and relationships with several lobbyists.

That was met with a security unit standing at the entrance of the senate chambers blocking the entrance of the four independent senators. Luke was smiling and he knew he had just won the war.

He immediately made a call to the Supreme Court Administrator and advised him of the actions of the Senate leadership. Three days later the court called a session and issued a direct order to the Senate that their blocking of the independent senators was a direct violation of the Constitution and that any bills passed during that time were then and there null and void.

When the public heard about it the revolt went in to full swing. Recalls were cropping up all over the place, everywhere you looked people were cutting any and all relationships with the current leadership of the senate. Four days later the four independent senators approached the doors to the chamber and they were opened for them.

They took their seats and business started. In just a few weeks the four independents had gone from also runs to masters of the forum. Luke sat at his desk with his briefcase on his lap, looking into it. There in the small box was that golden ball. He reached in and touched it and knew his days were numbered.

He looked around the chambers and sat back. He knew that what he had done was against all reason, but he had done it and he had the satisfaction of knowing that he had ended a lot of the abuse that had been going on in that chamber over the years.

He had two days left and knew that little was on the agenda for that day and the next so he decided to take a holiday and return home to await the inevitable.

Early the morning of the third day a gray car pulled into his driveway and continued to the circular approach to Luke's home. Two men got out and approached the door just as Luke opened it.

They stood there. "Are you the Senator?"

"Yes I am, and your names please.

"I'm Denton and my partner here is Felix."

"Gentlemen I would invite you in but what you're here for is messy and I chose not to get that mess all over in my house. If it's all right with you we'll do our business right here."

The two of them looked at one another and then back to Luke. "You know what we're here for?"

"Yes, I knew it two days ago."

"And, you did nothing about it?"

"No, this I have expected. The corruption in Washington is so deep that one man could never stop it, but what is going to happen here and now will bring about the total destruction of those who have sent you here. The government of this nation will never be the same again.

"Now do what you were sent here to do."

With that the two of them pulled their guns and pointed them at Luke and pulled the triggers.

Six months later two dozen FBI vehicles pulled up in front of the senate office building and special agents entered the building and went to ten specifically assigned offices. At each office they entered and requested to see the senator on the grounds of governmental necessity.

Ten minutes later they left the building with ten senators in custody and charged in the conspiracy of having Senator Luke Mann killed on the door step of his home six months earlier. Luke's rebellion was ended but he got the leaders of the sickness that permeated the senate of the United States.

As an off shoot of that action, the house found itself under direct investigation and a number of representatives were also arrested and charges were filed on various acts of criminal misconduct.

The two main party committees faced the same in-depth investigation and a number of upper managers and politicians were taken down as well...

Luke's gold ball was never seen again. Some claim it never existed and others claimed to having seen it and witnessing the changes in Luke as he took his hate and violent tendencies and turned them against the people that needed to be dealt with the most.

"You see Delbert, not all events are bad or good, they are events and each one is related to an individual who came to Duker's Store looking for something specific even if they didn't know what it was at first.

"Oh, and the Gold Ball? Well it's right here in the drawer where it has always been except for that short time when Luke needed it."

Chapter Six

Officer Thomas Handcock

I sat there watching Frank arrange some items on a shelf back of the counter. "Delbert, this place is history in the making. There are things here that go back all those years to the first day. Along with that is a varied supply of different happenings, as I said before, some good and some not so good.

"Have you noticed the golf club on the wall over there and here the ball in this little box and over here a diary that has been written in. All things here tell a story."

Delbert sat up and looked at Frank. "Wait a minute. Those are the items you told the stories about, how can they be here now if you sold them?"

Frank smiled at Delbert. "Son, when the people who buy these things are finished with them they come back here where they belong. Nothing sold out of this store stays away forever. As each life is finished with an item it comes back to us. Maybe someday in the future they will be sold again to another in need.

"That's the nature of Duker's Store; if something will work for one person then it will probably work for another."

I was looking at him and then it hit me. "What about the dynamite that you sold Dinky, it never came back?"

"No some items are what we call perishable. That is when they're used they no longer exist and will never return. But that is only about ten percent of our overall activity, so the majority of items come back."

I then turned and spotted a ballistic vest hanging on the wall. "What's the story behind that item?"

Frank turned and looked where I was pointing. "Oh Officer Thomas Handcock, yes, that was a particularly interesting situation.

145

...Officer Thomas Handcock was a police officer in his twelfth year of service. Up till then he was a model officer and was well liked by his fellow officers and the community in general.

I first met Thomas when he dropped into the store one afternoon. He was canvasing the Main Street stores in regards to a possible shoplifter that was working this area. I was in the back of the store when he came in."...

"You didn't meet him at the door like all the others?"

"No, he was not here for a need like the others. He was here providing a service and as a result I have no pre-arrival information on him.

...Anyway he came into the store and I heard the doorbell ring. I stepped out of the back room and there Thomas was looking at the vest on the wall."

"What's a vest like that doing here anyway? He asked."

"Oh that, well it's been here a long time now. I don't recall when we got it, all I know is that there had been a special request for one and here it is. The officer that wanted it never came to get it. I learned later on that he had been killed in a gun fight just the day before he was to pick it up.

"No one ever came for it and so there it sits waiting for whomever and whenever."

Thomas stood there looking at the vest. "That's an expensive vest and a good one as well. What do you want for it?"…

Delbert, I was looking at Thomas. He had now changed from being a service provider to me to a customer requesting a service from me, namely the vest in question. As soon as he said that I had this empty feeling enter my heart. "Delbert, you're not allowed to mitigate or get involved in a personal issue unless you are a part of it."

…I looked at Thomas. "Now you're sure you want to know what it costs."

He nodded his head. "Yes, I think I may buy it if the price is right."

I walked over and pulled the vest off the wall and laid it on the counter. Thomas walked over and started to look it over. "This is a top of the line vest. They come with everything. How much do you want for it?"

147

Finally I had to tell him. I had this heavy feeling that he shouldn't walk out of the store with that vest but my hands were tied. Even if I wanted to say something I couldn't. This was his destiny and I can't interfere in that. The rules are hard in that regard, I couldn't interfere. "That particular vest has never been used. When I got it, the value was six hundred fifty, right now it's on sale for four hundred fifty."

He stood there looking at it and finally reached into his back pocket. "Will you take a check in that amount?"

"Yes, your check, I'm sure, is good here."

He wrote the check and I gave him the receipt and he picked up the vest and headed for the door. He stopped at the door. "Oh by-the-way there has been a shoplifting gang working the downtown area. You need to be aware of that and watch out for them."

I thanked him and opened the door as he left, vest in hand.

Thomas walked out to his car and drove away heading back toward the police station just three blocks away. As he pulled into the parking lot he checked out of service and then took the vest and went into the station and then to the locker room.

In the locker room he took off his old vest and put the new one on, then put his uniform shirt back on and headed back to his car. He still had half a shift before his day was over. He was looking at a three day weekend

He had finished with the notification of the downtown stores and headed out to work the school zones for the afternoon school release. Up till that moment, he had been having a normal nothing ever happens day.

Those aren't bad days, it's just that they tend to drag along and seem to take twice as long to get through. All he had to do was work the school zone for speed violations while the kids were heading for home and then it was back to the office to finish doing a couple of reports and then heading for home and that long weekend.

He had no sooner set up for his speed monitoring when he heard it before he saw it. That particular car was well known to Thomas and the other police officers in the city and areas outside the city. The kid that drove that car had been cited more times than any group of fifty drivers trying to violate as many traffic laws as they could in a given time period.

Yeah, he knew that car by it sound well before he saw it. The owner, one Jeff Stanley, had built the car himself and he built it for speed. It was fast but it was also deadly. Jeff could build a car but he couldn't drive one worth beans.

As a result he thought he could outrun any police car in the county. Up till that time he had never been successful. You would have thought that he had figured that out by now, but he never did and this time it was no different.

Thomas would attempt to pull Jeff over for his speed and the usual pursuit would follow.

Sure enough here he came right through the middle of the school zone while children were present and he wasn't slowing for anything. The cross walk guard had to pull back onto the sidewalk and pull a couple of kids back with him. This time Thomas was taking Jeff for reckless driving.

Before Jeff got to where Thomas was parked Thomas turned on his red and blue overheads. That only made Jeff push his car that much harder. Thomas tried to wave Jeff over but as Jeff drove by he gave Thomas a derogatory salute and then sped off down the street.

Thomas took pursuit and notified dispatch that he was in pursuit of Jeff Stanley heading east on Beacon Street at a high rate of speed. He requested additional units to move in and assist in stopping Jeff.

This was the start of Thomas' last day and last hour of living. What would follow would be a battle seldom heard of or witnessed around those parts. Jeff Stanley was being his usual self that afternoon except there was one other issue involved. Jeff was planning on killing himself and he had planned a special kind of death.

Who knows what people are thinking when they're in a self-destructive mood, they're just not predictable and in this case no one would even come close to figuring out why Jeff did or what he was doing this time.

In the past Jeff would take the police on a short but lively run and then pull over and face the music, but on this day he seemed a little more aggressive and intense. After they had gone about five miles Thomas advised the other units working with him that there was something wrong or unusual about this pursuit.

He had dealt with Jeff enough to know that he was not a hateful person. He was the kind of guy that simply didn't give a damn and when he did something he would, in the end, faces the music and takes what was coming to him.

Not this time. No this time he was fighting and working to avoid and beat those pursuing him. As they progressed in the pursuit Jeff's actions became more and more aggressive and unpredictable. After ten miles Thomas considered dropping the chase and picking Jeff up later on a warrant.

Just then Jeff did something that meant that Thomas couldn't stop the chase. Jeff targeted a pedestrian standing at the curb watching the chase coming toward him. The man managed to dive out of the way breaking an arm while doing so.

Almost immediately Jeff then headed across the street and up into a lawn and targeted a man mowing his lawn. Jeff's car hit the lawnmower and knocked the man down fortunately not causing any injuries to the man but destroying the lawnmower.

Thomas knew then he had to get this kid stopped and it had to be sooner than later. He advised the other units of the situation and said that he would be hitting the car at the next intersection.

As Thomas moved up to the rear passenger quarter panel of Jeff's car, Jeff immediately slammed on his breaks making Thomas drive past him and putting the patrol car in a vulnerable position. Thomas swung right and away from Jeff and then applied his brakes in order to get back behind Jeff.

Just as he was passing Jeff's front passenger door he looked over at Jeff and Thomas was staring into the barrel of a revolver that Jeff was pointing at him.

Thomas saw Jeff pull the trigger twice and then the first round came through his window passing right in front of face right at the jaw level. The second round came in the window and hit Thomas in the neck passing through and out the window on the passenger's side.

He knew he had been hit and that he was in serious condition. He keyed his mic and tried to advise the other units of the situation and his condition. "All units subject just fired two shots at me. I've been hit in the neck. We need more help."

He heard several of the other units respond and then he started to feel light headed. He couldn't pass out now, they had to get this crazy dumb kid stopped and in custody before he kills someone.

By this time both sides of Thomas' uniform shirt were soaked in blood. He was trying to pull his own weapon out of its holster on his right side. When he got it out he stuck it out the window and opened up on Jeff's car. He concentrated on the rear window aiming toward the driver's position.

He could see Jeff pointing his gun back at the police car and pulling off rounds. He only had six rounds but the size of the weapon appeared to be large and if so they could do extreme damage to both the patrol unit and the officer.

Just then a second unit came up behind Thomas and pulled over and aligned with Jeff's car. That officer then stuck his weapon out the driver's window and opened up. The officer didn't hesitate, he hit Jeff's car with ten rounds as fast as he could pull the trigger. Two of the rounds hit the boy dead center in the back of his head.

He immediately fell over onto the seat of the car and the car started to slow. It moved to the right and then jumped the curb and hit a tree bringing the car to a stop.

Meanwhile Thomas was bringing his unit to a stop and managed to put it into park. As he sat there he could see units coming in from every direction and officers running toward Jeff's car and toward Thomas's unit.

His vision was starting to blur and he was having a hard time keeping his head up. It was then when his door opened and two hands reached in and popped his seatbelt loose and pulled him from the car and placed him on the ground.

Several officers had gathered around him and as he laid there he heard one say, "The little bastard is dead."

All that Thomas could think of was, damn I'm not going to have time to get my reports done. What the hell did that crazy little fool think he was doing?

Was he scared? Yeah, he was scared. He knew he was in bad shape and that there was a good chance that he was not going to make that three day weekend.

He heard the ambulance as it came racing into the scene. Within seconds hands

155

were picking him up and rushing him to the ambulance and then they were heading for the nearest hospital.

Funny, he had just bought one of the best body vests made and had put it on and then turned around and got shot in the neck. Hell of a lot of good that did him. Crap he had spent four hundred fifty dollars on the damn thing and it didn't do a thing for him.

As they pulled up to the hospital his vision was starting to fade. There was no more pain just a calm feeling that everything was going to be alright. He needn't worry about the reports or Jeff or anything else for that day. It all was going to be all right.

He knew he was going down a hallway as the lights in the ceiling were flying past. They passed through a door and then stopped in the middle of a room.

Hands were all over him as his clothes and that worthless vest was taken off of him. He could hear people talking and one of them asking him questions. "What was that question, I couldn't quite hear you? How can I answer if I can't hear you?"

Things were getting dimmer and he could no longer feel their hands on him or any pain from the wound for that matter. He was so tired all he wanted to do was close his eyes and rest. Slowly his eyes closed and then the sounds around him started to fade even more until there was silence and darkness.

One of the doctors working on the officer stepped back. "All right everyone he's gone. Close everything down and let the coroner know. Nurse record the time as four thirty-seven pm…

"Frank, you knew that the Officer was going to die didn't you. Even though he bought that vest, you knew?"

"Delbert, much of what happens in the store you will know about. Some will come in here with a bright future ahead of them while others will have no future at all.

"There's nothing you can do about it. Each individual must live their life to its final ending and you can say nothing or do nothing to alter or impact that ending, whatever it may be. You see that ending is hard wired. It's going to be no matter what you think, say or do."

Chapter Seven

Vince Sanders

"Delbert let me tell you about a man whose life would change more radically than any we have seen so far. His name is Vince Sanders and this man would change the world and all that we ever knew about it. Not only that, while making that change he would change as well, he would change in a way no other man had ever changed in his life.

"Not only will he change, but a close friend of his will face the same change and events that Vince faced. His name was Herald Gimble. Both men would face a moment of decision making that would impact all mankind and themselves in particular.

"See that flight helmet hanging there on the wall. That is the flight helmet that Vince came in here for and bought one day. In a way it never left this store, but that day he bought it and carried it out with him and when he had finished using it, it was back here, yet it always was hanging there.

"Confused, well believe me this story is as unbelievable as can be and once it is told you will understand what happened and how it impacted the world as a whole.

"Now I think it would best be told by Vince himself and so I will send you to that day and let him tell what happened to him after he bought that flight helmet."

Just then Delbert felt the room change and actually shift in its orientation. It seemed to have turned ninety degrees to the direction he had been looking. There standing before him was a vision of a man.

Frank reached out and touched Delbert's arm and whispered. "That is a projection of Vince. Don't ask me how it works or where it comes from, I don't know. All I can tell you is that from time to time it helps to know all the details of a specific event and this is one of them. Listen and pay close attention, it only happens once."

159

…For me speed was like a fine drug. It would race into my system like a stream of molten iron and drives me headlong into the desire for more, much more. Few people get the opportunity to drive a machine to its limits and when you do you go for it without any concern for what may or could happen.

You're totally consumed by the prospect of going faster, much faster, and that was why I was at the speed institute this early Friday morning. It was six o'clock on the twelfth of April, 2098. I had been contacted by my buddy Herald Gimble. Herald was a designer of machines, high speed machines that is. He had an insatiable appetite for designing and building anything that would go fast. And by fast I mean not in the normal realm of the meaning.

Whether on the ground, in the water, on the water, in the air, or in space, he wanted to build machines that would push the boundaries of science. Nothing was out of the question and everything was possible.

This time I would develop a strong feeling that Herald was crazy, nuts, out of his ever loving mind. This time he had decided that we could and would exceed the speed of light. Light, with a speed of one hundred eighty-six thousand miles per second, is the Universal speed demon and limit, and Herald was going to exceed it.

How fast is one hundred eighty-six thousand miles per second? Well consider the sun, which is ninety-three million miles away from Earth, its light can reach Earth in around nine minutes. At this point in time nothing, but nothing could go faster than light. In fact science had no idea what would happen if anyone were to exceed the speed of light.

Would they pass into another dimension or would they simply disintegrate? Maybe they would hit a flat wall, an unseen structure that no physical object could penetrate. Who knows? What I do know is that all of science tells you that nothing but nothing can go faster than the speed of light and Herald is saying that is exactly what he wants to do. Yet, the bigger part of this wacky idea is that he wants to include me.

Herald is about my age, maybe a little older. He is a tall six foot five inches and weighs around two hundred ten pounds. His hair is thinning, but still appears to be full and black. His eyes are a deep blue with a built in twinkle that tells you that this guy is just a little bit nuts.

He holds something like six degrees in varied fields with the highest being in physics. The man has more brains than a modern classroom. And this time he has gone all the way.

Well, Herald welcomed me and we went to his office and he presented his idea. The first question that came to my mind was. "Then what do you need me for?"

Dumb question! He wanted me to pilot the machine from the first test flight to the ultimate beyond light speed run. In other words my life was on the line. Yet, the idea of it was intriguing. Then Herald invited me to his shop.

It had no resemblance to any flying machine I had ever seen. One would expect to see a long slender tube of a body with some kind of airfoil on the sides and a tail section. Those would be for earth flight. After that, once in space the shape and layout meant nothing.

This thing was round, smooth and, well, plain round. Know what I mean, round, a ball. How else can I describe it? And, it was going to fly. It was going to fly faster than the speed of light.

All I could do was stand there and look at it. What could I say or how should I react. I guess I was dumbfounded. Herald put his hand on my shoulder. "Interesting isn't it?"

I looked at him like he was a moron or something. "Interesting? What the hell is it, a basketball?"

In actuality, it was not really a ball. I guess you could say it was three quarters of a ball. I'm not sure if it was the leading end or the trailing end that was the round ball layout. The rest of it was concave. That is, at the three quarter point of roundness, it stopped being round and become concave into the ball.

I would say the ball was probably forty feet in diameter. It appeared to be made of metal, probably aluminum or an alloy of aluminum. It was sitting in a cradle and a set of steps went up to the half-way point of the ball where there was a hatch standing open. There were lights on inside, but from my position I could not see into the ball.

Herald invited me up the stairs and into the ship. I had to go. This thing was so outrageous that I had to see what was inside.

As I entered the craft, I immediately noted the cockpit was designed for two people. I would not be flying this thing alone.

Once my eyes adjusted to the interior it staggered me. This cockpit was unlike anything I had ever seen or dreamed of for that matter. The overall area was bathed in a soft yellow light. The floor was a transparent material, probably a plastic of some kind.

The walls were covered with switches, buttons, gauges, meters, and video screens of every color, shape and size. Except the wall behind the flight seats, what I thought was the back wall and that was covered with a black fabric of some kind.

My eyes were drawn back to the floor and into the area under the floor. That area was bathed in a bluish light, soft and comfortable to the eyes. There was an egg shaped mass sitting in the middle of the floor in that area. Other than that there was nothing, just smooth floors and walls. I could hear a low hum coming from that location, but nothing else.

This thing screamed money. As far as I could tell everything in it was of the highest quality, there were things in there that were one of a kind and that meant money with a capital M. Herald was not funding this thing. He had a lot of money, but not this much.

I looked at Herald, "Two seats?"

He smiled, "Yeah, one for you and one for me."

He was going to be responsible for the power plant and its operation and I was the pilot. With something like this, what was there to pilot? As far as I could tell if I was doing one hundred eighty-six thousand miles a second, it would be in a straight line. Besides that, this thing was a ball and it was going to be more like a bullet than a high speed craft.

Herald walked over and sat down in the right hand seat and then motioned me to the left side seat. As I sat down I felt the firmness and yet comfortable quality of the seat. It rapped itself around me, but did so with a degree of firmness that supported every part of my body.

That made me wonder, what about the acceleration rate of this thing? I was sure it would not jump from zero to light speed in one step. This was going to be a long time, long range process in which the machine would accelerate at a constant rate until it hit its top speed and the only place it could do that was in space.

I took another look around and noted that there were no signs of food preparation facilities or bunks for sleeping.

Herald read my question before I could ask it. "There is no need for food or sleep. The achievement of our goal will be reached and we will return home in less than ten hours."

That stopped me in my tracks. "Herald, I'm not sure I'm your man for this job."

He held his hand up to stop me and told me that we should return to his office and he'll explain the whole thing to me at that time. As we left the ship I was feeling a little ill. This was far more than I had expected.

Once in his office he handed me a ream of paper and started to explain what he was planning and what my part in it would be.

Before we continued I set the papers down and looked at him. "Herald, why me?"

He stopped and leaned forward on his elbows and looked into my eyes. "You're the best pilot I know of, but even more important you are the most cautious and analytical pilot I have ever known. Those are qualities that this ship and flight need. Besides that I doubt if you could say no once you knew what this was about."

Then he started to explain in detail what the mission was. Now I'm not saying that I understood everything he said or was about to say. All I know is that he was trying to relate to me the design and concepts behind this machine in terms that I would understand and grasp.

"The target of our run will be the distance between Earth and Pluto. They have carefully designed a route across our solar system in order to miss as many hazards as possible. There was each planet and its moons, and the asteroid belt between Mars and Jupiter.

We would not be running on the plain of the planets, but at an angle of ninety degrees to the flatness of our solar disk. The rough distance between Earth and Pluto is three billion seven hundred million miles. In that course he expected to reach light speed in one billion miles and then go for the super light speed in the second billion miles and the third billion miles to slow down so that we could make the turn around.

167

On the way back we would use the same procedure so that we could record a two way speed qualification."

I sat there looking at him. "Well, how will we know if we achieve light speed and then surpass that?"

"Vince, we won't, the machine will record that. We will know that we achieved light speed when we get to the end of the course and look at the timing records. It will be the same on our return."

About that time I felt a pain go through my chest. "And, what if we hit something going either way, what then?"

"We won't know that either, I can assure you that you will feel nothing what-so-ever. It would just be over in a flash."

"Herald, would we feel the acceleration?"

He started nodding his head. "At first we would but as the ship increased in speed that sensation would go away as well. For all intents and purposes we would be sitting there just as we are now in this office. The only indication of speed would be the metering gauges in the wall in front of us. That is until we hit the light barrier and then I have no idea what we will feel or sense."

168

I sat there listening to him and thinking about that very issue. "Herald, you know that throughout all of science there is a rule that nothing, but nothing can exceed the speed of light. As far as I know, that has not changed in any way."

Herald then stated that was the risk of this project. However, science has also determined that at one time as the universe came into existence its expansion did surpass the speed of light that was called Inflation. That means that the speed of light can be passed and we're going to do it.

He and others felt that under the right circumstances, light speed could be exceeded. However, he needed the best pilot he could find, one that he personally could depend on and that was me.

As I sat there I knew that this thing was probably the most dangerous situation I have ever ventured into. In fact at that moment I felt that I was looking at a suicide situation. I was sure this was not possible and that we would end up a spot of vapor floating around in space.

Finally I leaned back and looked at Herald and nodded my head. He smiled and thanked me. "Vince, we will come back from this, we will achieve our target."

I had a week before I needed to be on line and working into the system. During that week I cleared up all my personal needs and made a run back to my home town. While there I stopped in at a place called Duker's Store looking for a new flight helmet. I found the exact helmet I needed and bought it and headed back to Utah and my new job. That's an odd store in that everyone I talked to would say that they have everything or anything you want or need right there, and they were right.

Six months later I found myself sitting in the pilot's seat of the sphere preparing to launch. Unlike other objects that were sent into space, we were not on the high end of a rocket. The sphere was capable of launching itself into space.

The roof of the work shop had been opened and we were finishing our final count down in the launch. Needless to say I was in the pilot's seat of the most advanced flying vehicle the world had ever seen, but at this time had not seen the sphere, but in fifteen minutes it would.

After accepting Herald's offer we started the training process. Physically I was in great shape, but Herald assured me that it did not matter. The sphere would move us from Earth's surface into orbit with little or no discomfort.

Then I learned about the inner workings of the sphere. The egg on the floor below us was in fact the engine that would drive this vchicle into our destiny. The power this thing was capable of was beyond even the wildest of dreams of all the technology this world had ever developed and built. The fact is there were no moving mechanical parts in the engine. It was all energy. An energy of the type no man had ever unleashed before and with this would come a degree of hazard for us all, even unto the universe.

The theory of light speed had been addressed by Einstein in his Theory of Relativity. In that theory rested all the elements of time travel, the creation of energy and the exploration of space. We were going to try and violate that theory by breaking the light speed barrier. Who knew what would happen.

Though I had never seen inside the engine cowling of this ship, I had felt the

171

power of it while we were testing it out. There is a feeling that comes from the inner most depths of your soul when that engine starts up. You know you are listening to something that is so far and away ahead of anything else that it is downright scary.

And now, six months later we are loading up and preparing for our first test flight into the upper atmosphere. We were not going into space yet. We were just going to test the ships power capabilities. Due to its overall design, it is not designed to fly at any significant speed in our atmosphere. Yet, it still needed to achieve a minimum speed of seventeen thousand miles an hour in order to move into orbit. It was going to be interesting.

At eight hundred hours the hold downs on the ship's cradle were released for the first time. The ship was rotated so that the concave rear was facing down and we were reclined in our flight seats. At the direction of the control center I shoved the ship throttle forward and we lifted off.

The first thing I realized was that I only needed a slight percentage of the throttle, maybe a quarter of an inch. This thing had power coming out of its butt like nothing I had ever flown before.

We cleared the building roof and gave the ship a second charge of throttle and she leaped ahead so fast it scared me. I almost throttled all the way down, but controlled myself and let her take her head. We passed supersonic in less than five seconds and I never felt a thing. On top of that the ship seemed to slip through the atmosphere like it was greased. There was absolutely no feeling of acceleration, nothing. I wasn't even pushed back in my seat. That was strange.

I looked at Herald and he nodded. Finally I voiced my question. "Herald, what the hell is going on? No 'G' forces at all!"

Herald looked at me again. "Vince, I was not sure what would happen. All my calculations told me that this machine would generate a force shield that would envelope the ship, but I was not prepared for the power of the field. It's off the charts."

"Herald, where did this technology come from? I mean I have never heard of or seen anything like this." I was sure I had not been told the whole story on this ship and its engine. "This ship could be shaped like a cube and it would still fly faster and be more maneuverable than anything else flying today."

"Vince, I can't tell you everything at this point, but, I can tell you that this technology was Earth born. Once we're in space and making our run, I'll fill you in on everything.

We completed the test flight and had landed back at the building. As we left the ship I felt the sides of it and they were cool. Almost as if we had never left the ground.

Herald smiled and headed for his office. I had to find a stiff drink and fast.

We were only three weeks from the launch of our attempt to exceed light speed when I finally decided I needed a clearing of the minds with Herald. I got to his office and sat down. He looked at me and knew I was deeply bothered. "What is it?"

I looked at him and told him that I had never once in all the years that we have been friends ever felt that I could not trust him, until now. "Herold, there was too many things going on that did not fit the picture of what we were doing. I was beginning to think the whole light speed thing was a fake and that something else was going on I had better know about before this thing goes one inch further."

There was a long and quiet pause. "Vince, this thing is so big that we all get lost in it from time to time. I know that I have not been giving you the entire story on what we are doing, but it was my hope you would trust me all the way. I have never meant to deny you the information you needed to do the job, but I have kept some things from you. Well a whole lot of things from you.

"First off, this is an attempt to exceed light speed. That is fact. Second, we need to exceed light speed for one vital reason and that is the survival of the world. Not just the people, but the whole physical world, this place we call Earth. Now the question is how do the two relate?

"The problem came up five years ago. A group of astronomers were watching a large star and its adjoined planets as it moved through space. After several months of tracking this star they determined that it was heading right at us. That star was around fifty years away from us. After further evaluations they determined this on coming star is about five hundred times the size and mass of our sun.

"Vince, that means trouble for the whole solar system. If that thing gets here and even has a wide miss margin, it will destroy this entire solar system. The question that came up was how do we stop it or, can we even slow it down?

"That set us on a five year task of developing something that could impact the coming system and either move it or destroy it before it gets to within a light year of us. That is where Heaven's Gate comes in. Yeah, that's the project name for this little ship.

Now your next question is, "How can a ship this size impact a star that is five hundred times the size and mass of our sun?" And, my answer to you is that it can. That is the reason for the faster than the speed of light issue.

"Our current theory is that if we hit that star with an object that is moving in excess of light speed, and in this case we believe we will be moving around three times the speed of light when we get there, we will hit with such mass and speed that it will literally move that star as much as a million miles off its current course. Either that, or it will nova and take out its entire solar system.

"It's currently forty-five years away and we plan on being there in no less than ten hours when we hit it. She will pass by our solar system by a factor of ten times the diameter of our solar system. This is a onetime try and if we fail then everything else is gone. We cannot move ten billion people out of the way. It just can't happen."

As I sat there the magnitude of this project suddenly hit me. But, what really hit home was the term he used; "if we hit that star."

That hit home big time. "Herald, are you telling me this is a one way trip for you and me? Is that the reason you did not tell me the whole truth, was that what you planned on doing after it was too late to stop it? That you were committing suicide, but in my case you're willing to murder me?"

He leaned back in his chair with a look of shock on his face. "Vince, I had no intention of doing that. It was just that I thought it better to wait until we were into the actual project and then tell you. I now realize that it was not wise and that it was wrong. Yes, this is a one way trip."

The anger came on fast, but reversed just as fast. I could see in Herald's face he was being honest with me. The load on him must be huge. We sat there for maybe five minutes before I finally leaned forward and told him that I was in. I had no one to worry about. No wife, children, parents, brothers or sisters or any other close family. I was an ideal choice for this mission.

On the other hand, I knew Herald had a family. His wife Mary was a gem and he had three children. "What about your family Herald?"

He lowered his head and told me he had not told them anything about this project. Mary thought it was just another one of my aerodynamic projects and nothing more. "Vince, this has been the most closely guarded secret the world has ever had. Outside of you, me and the governing board, no one knows about what we are doing.

"Vince, it must remain that way. We cannot afford to have anything go wrong now. We have three weeks to go and we cannot afford any goof ups. You have to keep this to yourself no matter what."

"Herald, it will be life as usual. I will live my days just as I have. Nothing will change."

When I walked out of Herald's office I knew that the next three weeks were going to be the hardest I had ever experienced. We had hours of testing and preparation work ahead of us. Even the ships support personnel were not aware of what was happening. They just knew that we were on a march to break the light barrier and nothing else.

The next two weeks I spent working like a mad man toward the record try. Stan, one of the lead flight managers, was working with me in the cockpit one afternoon when he asked me. "What happens when you go through the barrier?"

I looked at Stan. "I have no idea."

"Don't you worry about what could or may happen?"

I smiled at him. "Yeah, I do. It's just that there is no way to know what will happen so why worry about it."

"Are you afraid?"

"A little, as a matter of fact the closer I gets the tighter I feel. But, once we get started I won't have time to think about it. I'm sure that if it's bad, we'll be going so fast that we won't even know what happened."

Stan leaned back and looked at me. "Man you must be crazy or something."

"Yeah, or something." I responded.

We worked on the prep work for the next hour without saying anything. As we completed the task at hand Stan stepped over to me and offered his hand. I took it and he said that he would pray the best for us. I thanked him and walked away. Wish I could have told him more about this thing, but that was not possible.

The final day came. I was up early and at Heralds office by five hundred hours. Most everything was done and when I walked in Herald was finishing what appeared to be a letter. I did not ask but assumed that it was a letter to his wife. He licked the envelope and placed it on his desk. As we left the office he told his secretary. "If we fail to return, give that letter on my desk to my wife."

The secretary assured us we would return, but she would do as he wished if we did not.

It was a long lonely walk to the main building that morning. The sun was just coming up over the mountains to the east. The air was light and crisp and there was a smell of salt in the air. Working at a facility that is located on the salt flats in Utah State will have that smell early in the morning hours.

The flight crew was standing by Heaven's Gate as we entered the building. The roof had already been opened and all was ready for the speed attempt. There was a sense of excitement, but there was a sense of suppressed fear as well. Everything had been done. We had checked, double checked, and triple checked everything. Nothing had been left out, nothing.

I was the first through the hatch into the cockpit followed closely by Herald and then the two-man prep team who would assist us in getting into our seats and buckled down. That took ten minutes and then the hatch was closed.

All pre-flight checks were completed and everything was green light and go. Herald started the engine start sequence and it came on line in seconds. He had all greens and we then set the countdown for takeoff. At the ten second mark I had a huge hole in my gut that told me this was the real thing and we would be leaving this place for the last time.

Lift off was uneventful. At that point the president would be walking into the congressional chamber to give an important announcement to congress, the nation, and the world. At the time we cleared the atmosphere he started his announcement. When he finally related the facts of the situation I had hit the acceleration sequencer and we were off.

We passed the moon in less than five minutes as we started to pick up speed. Again, there was no sense of acceleration other than watching the screens and seeing the Earth fall away behind us. We were approaching the barrier, and this was the moment of truth. If we made it, the next stop, literally, would be the opposing star some forty-three years away.

Our estimates were that we would reach our target in about ten hours. In that time we would be working hard, lining ourselves up for the impact on the star with such force that nothing in the universe had ever been seen like this before.

Any object of any size moving at the speeds we would be moving at carried with it such power and force that nothing could withstand it. Not even a star five hundred times the mass of our sun.

As we approached ninety-five percent of light speed a slight vibration was felt in the machine. I looked down through the floor at the engine and was sure I could see a slight glow coming from it. Other than that it was operating at optimal levels and showing no signs of difficulty. The barrier was coming at us so fast that I did not even notice when we went through it. No crash, noise, shaking, bumping, nothing. The total effect was a change in what our external camera observations were.

Space was gone. I mean the space as we knew it; full of stars, galaxies, nebulas, etc. What was in its place was a flux of lights and shadows. Almost like when they put the color pigment in a bucket of paint and the shapes and blending that you see when the mixing starts.

By the time I managed to look over at the clock I realized we had cleared the outer limits of our own solar system and were entering deep space. It suddenly dawned on me that if we hit anything other than the star we were targeting, we would never know it. I looked to Herald. "How fast are we going?"

Herald's eyes were as big as a dish when he looked back and said that he thought we were around twice the speed of light at that point and still accelerating.

"God, that's three hundred seventy-two thousand miles a second and increasing. Is there a limit to that?" I asked.

"I don't know. This is all new to me too."

For the first time I was really getting scared. It was crawling all over me, but what the hell could I do about it now. Then I noticed something. I was looking at my hands when I noticed one of my age spots, you know those brown pigment spots that appear on the back of your hands as you get older, was going away. Really, it was getting smaller and smaller right before my eyes.

"Herald, look at your hands."

He looked at me and then down to his hands and sat there watching the age spots recede and disappear.

He looked over at me. "What the hell?"

He then grabbed his notebook and started writing a number of things down, then looked over at me, "Time reversal."

"You have got to be kidding."

He was smiling and nodding his head. "No, that is what is happening. When we crossed that barrier we also went into a different time system. Time as we know it is based on the speed of light. Once you leave that system time will either increase or decrease. We were not sure just what it would do. We are getting younger. So if we were to slow below the barrier would we go back to our age before we entered it?"

Herald did not have the answer. Anyway it made no difference, we were on course and impact was just eight hours away.

The next seven hours we spent watching ourselves getting younger. That was crazy. In that seven-hour period I had regressed back to around age forty-two, when we started, I was fifty-nine. Herald checked our speed calculations again and determined we were around four times the speed of light.

The clock was moving relentlessly toward the impact time, forty-five minutes to go. At this rate we would hit the star at around six times the speed of light. Not knowing what was going to happen, it had been determined that we would remain at our collision speed until we were sure we had cleared the outer planets of the solar system we were targeting.

At that point we would start our deceleration procedure, assuming that we survived the impact, and bring our ship, Heaven's Gate to a stop in space, beyond the target star and its related solar system.

We knew it when we hit the star. It was a sudden jab, like being hit in the shoulder by a buddy during a game. You know, a friendly punch, except that this was jaw busting quick and sharp. What had just happened we had no idea? We had to have hit the target; all the indicators and measurements confirmed that.

Yet we were still accelerating. This thing just would not stop.

Herald figured out how much further we had to go before going sub-light again. Finally we were there. I set the throttle to reverse and let the ship to start a gradual slow down. Coming out of super light speed is more violent than going into it, but we made it without any damage or injuries.

Herald immediately brought the rear looking cameras into view and what we saw was beyond anything I could even began to relate in a logical and understanding manner, but I'll try. In the place where the danger star should have been was a super nova. The entire solar system of that giant star had novae. There was nothing left. Earth would see the explosion forty-two years from now and we were right on top of it. In fact we had caused it.

Then it dawned on me that we could not go back the way we came. The retracing of our route was out of the question. We could not get into super light speed before we reached the nova. I looked at Herald and he smiled. "We figured that into our system. If we survived the hit, then they set the system up to take an alternate return route and head for home."

He brought the computer on line and started the navigation sequence and then sat back.

I could feel Heaven's Gate turning and then starting its acceleration. We were ten hours out from home and in that time, we will have seen Earth move about eighty years in time and our own age will have gone back to around twenty-two years old. Herald would return a spry twenty-five years old.

As we came out of super light speed we were back within our own solar system and passing beyond the asteroid belt. It was then that Herald realized that Mary would be gone and that his children were either quite old or had passed on as well.

So goes the price of saving a solar system from utter destruction. We didn't even know if the Earth would remember us or not. We had no idea what the political situation would be or if our nation even existed anymore. In effect we were aliens coming into an alien world for the first time. What would they think?

We passed the moon one hour out from Earth. As we passed by we noted a number of lights on the surface and other vehicle activities moving between Earth and the Moon. Herald started the automatic hailing system to alert Earth that we were returning. It was hoped that they were still monitoring our frequency when a voice came over it. "Attention alien craft please state your intentions and origin."

Herald looked at me like he had just been caught with his hand in the cookie jar, "Alien, Intentions, and Origin?"

I picked up the mic and started reciting the prescribed dialog we had planned on using if we returned. "Earth base, Heaven's Gate returning from Demon Star mission, request permission to land Utah base."

There was a long wait and then a question. "Is Herald Gimble on board?"

"Yes, this is Vince Sanders Pilot."

Again there was a long wait and then a voice returned. "Welcome home gentlemen we have a lot of questions."

"I'm sure you do." I replied.

As we came into the field on the salt flats of Utah we were met by a flight of crafts that were totally unknown to us, as was our craft to them. We landed exactly twenty-one hours from the time we left Earth eighty-three years prior. We were both in our mid-twenties looking nothing like we did when we first left twenty-one hours ago. We had our whole lives ahead of us.

The fact that we became younger as we traveled through hyperspace at super light speed had not been anticipated. So now we had our lives to live over again. I don't know if I'm ready for that, but I'll take a whack at it.

Herald was faced with trying to find his grandchildren and great grandchildren and to learn of his wife Mary and how her life went after he left.

The Super Nova of the destroyed Demon Star would not be seen for another forty-two years or so. It would be a huge hole in the sky and few would really know the true story.

Heaven's Gate was moved off into an old hanger to be held there for future evaluation. Their current drive systems were the same as hers except they were an upgraded generation ahead of her. Earth had long since moved into space travel and had been colonizing other star systems and planets for some fifty years.

We both received our pensions, which were compounded over the eighty-three years we were gone making us both independently wealthy. Yep, the rest of my second life was going to be just fine. I was around twenty-two years old and had actually lived a total of one hundred forty-five Earth years thanks to Heaven's Gate.

I turned to Herald. "Well Herald, you take care of yourself and good luck in finding everyone. I really do hope it all works out for the best for you."

Herald offered his hand. "Vince, I wish the same to you. Enjoy your new life and this time, make something of yourself."

I took his hand and laughed. "I'll do that Herald. See ya someday."

Herald laughed. "You too Vince, good luck."

Yes, I always have loved the smell of the early morning hours of the day. The sun was just coming up over the mountains to the east, the smell of the salt from the flats here in Utah were there just as I remembered them...

"Frank, you're telling me that things can happen in the future here at Duker's Store?"

"Delbert that is not what I am saying. I am saying that time has no place here in the store. When you enter, you enter in relationship to your time and not the time of others. Somewhere in time Vince entered the store and bought the flight helmet for his coming experience. When that was over the helmet returned to Duker's Store and there it is on the wall as it always has been and always will be except for one 21 hour period when it was needed."

By now I was more than a little confused. I had just experienced an event that either had taken place in the past or was going to take place sometime in the future, which I was not sure of.

Somehow, I had been selected to take over the store when Frank determined he wanted to retire. I had no idea what that entailed but over the past several hours I had learned much more than I realized. I guess the issue I was faced with was the fact I was going to take over the store and I had little or no choice in it.

"Frank tell me this, when you retire what are you going to do with yourself?"

He sat there looking at me. "Delbert, the term retire is relevant. From your perspective you visualize me sitting on a beach or in some far off place passing time.

"I'm afraid that visual idea is wrong. For me retirement means I will retire from operating the store. I have lived in this place for many years. The truth is I have been here for almost two hundred years.

"When it is time for me to turn this place over to you I will remain at that point when I release the store to you. One second you and I will be making the switch and the next second you will be here minding the store for however long you're meant to be here."

"Frank, are you telling me you're going to die at that point?"

"No, listen to me Delbert. Time is the strangest concept man has ever faced. No, a second is a second unto itself. Each second has its place in the time continuum but that point is not stationary. Time flexes and each second can be anywhere it need be while still maintaining its place when that second was created.

"Delbert, I will be as that second. I can remain in the continuum or I can move off to another point while still holding my place in the overall continuum. For me the adventure of life will just be starting. For me I will be able to go as I please and do as I please. There will be no place, no time that I will be denied access to.

"That my friend is the ultimate in adventure. My life will continue unabated by the physicality of this place called Earth.

"I have put my time in at Duker's Store, and now I will take my time and live it as I wish and where I wish. I am one of but a few, as you will be one day who will have free movement through the time continuum. That is my reward for my time spent here.

"Now we need to take a look at another event that someone else lived through. You're almost to the point of achieving total control of Duker's Store."

Chapter Eight

Steven Neely

"Delbert we are going to make another time jump. This time you will know the time and witness what took place. I want you to see that the continuum here in Duker's Store is flexible and will run the range as each need comes through that door.

"This time we will be dealing with a man that has fallen into a game of cat and mouse and if he is successful he will live and if not, well he will pay the ultimate price."

Steven came into the Store looking for camera equipment. As he entered the store and the door closed I felt the move to his actual time on the continuum. He was living in 2159 and he had developed a plan for instant wealth. However, he needed a camera and he happened to come into Duker's Store to try and find the right camera.

The fact was he had no idea just what kind of camera and support equipment he needed for the job he was planning. Obviously he needed Duker's Store and the camera and equipment that were waiting here for him.

As soon as we shook hands I knew what he was doing and the fact that it was not legal. Again, that is not my or your place to judge or refuse to supply his needs. This is his life and he will live it and pay the consequences whatever they may be, good or bad.

The fact was that Duker's Store had the camera and related equipment there on the shelves waiting for him, the exact equipment he would need to carry out his plan, if he survived. So let's see what it was that Steve got himself into.

…Gees, how could I have done that? It was perfect and then I took one step too many and now I'm about to pay for it with my life. Everything had been worked out to the second and it was going great. There was no way I could screw this one up, but I did, me and my perfection mode. All I wanted to do was make it just one touch better and that was the undoing of the whole thing.

It seems like it was maybe three months ago that the idea came to me. At first it sounded like a stupid idea, but the more I thought about it the more logical and doable it became. The point was it was so simple anyone should have seen it, yet I was the only one.

It was one of those hit and miss situation that found me in the right position looking from the right perspective when I realized what I had sitting in front of me. Not only could I make a killing this time, but no one and I mean no one would or could ever know. If I did this right it would take seconds and I would be set for life. If I screwed up, my life would be just seconds.

I knew exactly what needed to be done and started to think out all the little ifs, ands, and buts to make sure that I was moving in the right direction and that in fact this thing was as fool proof as it appeared to be. That is as fool proof as it can be until this fool came along.

The time was a beautiful summer day in the month of August 2159. The usual haze was drifting across the sky, as it did every morning around this time. Traffic was light and the noise levels were down for that time of day. I don't know. It was one of those perfect days that seem to be far and few between in this day and age.

Here in Brownsville the bulk of the people commute to the big city for their jobs. The city is just twenty-five miles away and it only takes around ten minutes to get from this station to the main terminal in the city. Besides, living outside of the city in a place like Brownsville just made life that much better.

The workers shuttle had just left the station and there were fewer than a dozen people still on the platform. Most of them were maintenance people cleaning up after the masses had finally cleared the station. The next shuttle would not be coming in and moving out for the next twelve hours. In effect it was a dead zone at this time of the morning.

As I sat there and watched the others carrying on with their usual daily activities I began to realize that few if any of them were even aware of me being there on that bench right smack dab in the middle of the station platform. As they worked around me not a single one spoke or even acknowledged that I was there, not a one.

That's when I noticed the actions of the personnel working on the platform. They don't see me. Or, if they see me, they don't care or have time to consider me. I sat there for the next few minutes and watched each and every one of them as they finished up their varied duties and started moving off the platform and off into the greater station area. In a rather short period of time I was left totally alone with not another soul in sight.

It was then that I noted, in amazement, the tag counters at the gates had been left wide open. Now tag counters are devices that accepts and credits each citizen's tag as they pass through the gates heading for the shuttles.

When your tag is recognized and counted it automatically deducts the fare costs from your account. This happens in just seconds so that the crowd can pass on through the gates without slowing down. There must be access to hundreds of millions of markers through each one of those tag counters, and they are standing there wide open.

Now a tag is a rather simplistic piece of equipment. Basically it is a bracelet that one wears, on either wrist. As you pass near a reader or pass over the gating plate, the reader will recognize and read your tag and then carry out the transaction automatically. You don't have to think, hold your wrist up, slow down, or anything. Just pass over the plate and it happens as fast as the crowd can move to the shuttle.

The significant thing about the reader is that they are nearly impregnable. That is you would need a significant amount of time to tear one open and in that time you would be laying there with a dozen bullet holes in you. They are not a piece of equipment you will be able to force entry into.

Second, they are shielded. That is they are protected from electronic snooping and the only way you could electronically gather any information from them would be by getting into them. That is why finding a whole line of readers standing wide open is so unbelievable.

The financial structure across the country is set up so that tag readings are automatically processed for each and every citizen. All account records are stored in a massive facility in the middle of the country. Every banking transaction, every stock transaction, every mortgage transaction, every new or used vehicle transaction and so on are recorded at this center and charged to or deposited to the individuals account. Nothing and I mean nothing is transacted outside of that system. Even friend to friend or garage sales transactions are recorded.

Everything is handled with the marker system. There is no real cash on hand. I think real money methods were dropped like twenty-five years ago. If anyone comes up with any old money it is immediately confiscated by the government and destroyed. All transactions are handled through tag readers and tag bracelets are worn by every citizen. So, anytime you see a means of accessing the governments system from the outside, it is monumental and this was.

I thought to myself, "All a person needs do is walk by those open tag counters with a transfer tag and you could move millions from the tag accounts of the transportation system into any account you desired. And, it all would happen in seconds. I mean seconds.

200

So fast that one person could cover the distance of all the tag counters in less than thirty seconds and each and every independent transfer would take place. No, all you needed to do was access just one of the readers, not all of them."

It dawned on me that I would need to have a place to drop those transfers and that it would have to be a secure location, one that could not be traced in any way or manner. With that I realized this had to be impossible. All electronic transfers or transactions were immediately recorded and reported to the central banking computer located in the center of the nation.

Yet, there had to be a way and I was going to find it.

I figured I needed to move rather quickly on this in that some inspector or others may come along at any time and recognize the situation and correct it and I would be out. I had a lot to think about and do in the next couple of days. Being one to never pass up a good deal I decided then and there to go for it.

That afternoon I went to the central data storage facility and started looking into the digital tag management system that was used across the country. In that system each citizen was provided with an identification bracelet that was imbedded with the individual's personal information including their financial management system and their account activities and levels. It was really a rather complex and powerful system.

Basically a person could walk into a store and carry out their normal shopping procedure and when they found an item they wanted they placed it in their tote-bag and carried it away. As they exited the store the tag reader would recognize the tag on each item in the tote-bag and would then register the transaction to the purchasers account and all was done. Charge tags on the items being purchased could not be removed until the item had been charged against someone's tag. As you can see the tag reader was the key to this entire system.

These readers were never left open and unattended at any time even if it was felt they were fool proof and had perfect security. Perfect security, you and I know there is no such thing. But, the mere fact no one ever got away with trying to cheat a tag reader gave them an air of perfection. My job was to work around and behind that façade and take advantage of what happened each morning on the platform at the transit station.

Right up front I knew that if I queered this, I would probably pay for it with my life. The governing body would see to that, no one, but no one jerked the government around and lived to talk about it later on. The risks were high, but the payoff was beyond calculation. I simply had to try.

Yet, I still had to consider the fact that this could have been a onetime occurrence and that tomorrow it would not be so. With that I determined that I needed to be there again tomorrow and the next day and so on till I was sure this was a normal operation.

There was a second reason and that was to have them get used to seeing me at the station each morning at that time. I had to figure out some reason for being there that was harmless and boring as hell.

I went back the next day and took a book and a pad and pencil with me and sat down on the bench facing the reader line and started to read my book. The morning passed and people came and went until the early morning flood of commuters was over. Sure enough as the last of the commuters cleared out the staff at the station moved down the reader line opening all the readers and leaving them unattended. Why, for what reasons were they doing this? I had to find out, it was vital to my plan.

I needed a way to move closer to the reader line and still not call undue attention to myself. Too much attention and the security unit would be on me like flies and then I would be in real trouble.

It was then, as I sat there thinking about how I would set myself up there in the station, that I knew I needed to carry my plan out without being a concern to anyone who passes through or works there. My eyes fell on the shadows that were cast on the floor of the station waiting area. So, as I sat there looking at them something told me that those shadows were my ticket to this place for as long as I wanted or needed to be here.

I looked up and noticed the structure of the roof and that gave me my idea. So, I became an artist. I would need cameras, lights, note pads, and drop cloths for my new career. This whole idea was brilliant.

You have to see one of these commuter stations in order to understand my reason for becoming an artist. These stations were not open air stations. They were under glass and were protected from the harmful effects of our sun.

In the last fifty years or so the climate here on earth had changed considerably due to changes in our atmosphere. The effects of the sun have been multiplied by the numbers and types of greenhouse gases that have found their way into the atmosphere.

So, an attempt is made by the government to enclose as much of our environment as possible to cut down on the harmful effects of the sun. This station is no different. Yet, the attempt to provide this protection would give me the means for becoming an artist.

It was the structure of the dome that would become my reason for being there. Not the dome itself, but the shadows that were cast by the sun as its light passed through the superstructure of the dome and the glass itself.

The design of the structure of the dome was two layered. The outer structure was made up of steel beams and girders that formed a lattice effect on the outside. The interesting thing about this lattice layout was that it was not made up of straight lines, but had curves and intersecting lines between the curves and straight line designs.

From this structure they hung a second lattice layout that encased the many glass panels that enclosed the station area that I was working in. Each glass panel was shaped differently and set into the lattice at different and precise angles so that the sun light would pass through and cause any number of different patterns and colors on the floor below. It was this color and pattern layout that I used as my artistic purpose in this station.

It would be these patterns and colors that would give me the reason to move freely around the station proper and in that process around the tag reading line. My plan was set and I showed up the next day ready to become the artist that I have never been.

I walked in with my bag slung over my shoulder. I had a camera and several pads and numerous pencils both color and black. I was ready and figured that if nothing else I could get a few good pictures anyway.

Just the process of getting the camera and equipment for it was an adventure in itself. Fortunately there is a store here in Brownsville that had everything I wanted and I was able to get everything for a reasonable price, now I was ready to use them.

As before, the crowd came and went and the station staff moved down the tag reader line opening each reader as they passed by. By this time I had my pads and camera out and had already started looking at and setting up my process in selecting different light patterns for my projects.

This brought the attention of the station staff on me, but it was something I needed to work through. I made a point of asking one of the staff if there were any restrictions in my moving around the station while selecting shadow shapes and taking my photos. They advised that I needed to stay away from the tag reader line, but otherwise I was alright to go anywhere in the public area of the station.

So it started. Day after day I worked the shadow game and day after day I moved closer to the tag reader line. In just a few days I noted the staff was again oblivious to my presence and I stuck to my schedule I had worked out so carefully. I would always be there ten minutes before the end of the commuter rush and then start my aimless wandering around looking for new and unique shadows cast by the dome of the station.

It took me four weeks to be able to move to within a reasonable distance from the tag reader line. I needed to be within three feet of the line in order to try to determine why they left them open and get a good idea as to the layout of the reader equipment inside the cabinet.

It worked. As I took my photos I also carried a scanner that scanned the makeup of the interior of the reader cabinet. I noted the reason for opening the units was because of heat, plain simple heat dissipation. During the commuter rush the readers were working overtime and they tended to heat up.

As with any electromagnetic device heat was a killer and their way of saving on the maintenance of these readers was to give them a cooling off period after each rush. I wondered if the same was true at the evening rush some twelve hours later. I made a mental note to check that out.

Now, I had one other problem to work on and that was the tag bracelet I wore. Everyone had to wear a tag bracelet, it was the law. So, whenever you got to within a few feet of a tag reader it would recognize you and there would be a record of your being at that place at that time and date.

It was no great problem getting an inert bracelet so I could work close to the tag readers without registering my presence. Where the danger came in was if I drew the attention of the security unit while I was wearing an inert bracelet. They carry portable readers with them and when they approach you they read your tag bracelet. To have a read come back blank would result in my being belted down in an interrogation chair and getting my brain scrambled for the next three hours while they try to figure out who I was.

No I needed to be boring and so drab and unimportant no matter where I was in the station or what I was doing. That, in the end would be the key to the whole master plan I was hatching. In addition I learned to move around the station with my active bracelet on without activating the readers.

Then it dawned on me I needed to activate one of them every now and then just to show I was there and I would normally come within the range of the readers. It was all part of getting them accustomed to my being present and working there. When the time came for me to move in on the readers and carry out my plan I would need to wear the inert bracelet.

Now, I knew what the problem was. The tag readers were overheating and instead of dealing with the issue the station master determined that he could cool them down by leaving them open for a few hours after each rush and save on any repair costs. Perfect, it was the door to my becoming wealthy and boy was it coming.

Being somewhat of a techie I knew that I needed a tag transfer card in order to be able to move the tag money from the transit authorities banking accounts to my own private and hidden account and that was going to be a real nut buster of a job. Getting the cards was not a problem, but getting the coding and the transfer location was going to be a task, but a doable one.

I needed to build the card and then do a test run. That, from my perspective would be the most dangerous part of this escapade. First I needed an account system so that the markers would move out of the authorities account and into a system that would move it across the country and back a number of times until such time that it could be diverted and disappear off the system.

That was done all the time by the larger corporate groups in the country and by organized crime elements as well. The key to the game was to stay low key at all times.

I knew the government did not keep their funds in the national banking system in the middle of the country. Their system was an off shoot of that and was dedicated just to the government. Any activity on that system had to have government passwords and identification. The readers held that information for me. That would give me the access I needed to the accounts so that the tag reader could transfer and deposit the funds into the account I wanted them to.

I also needed an account that would not show the sudden growth when the authorities markers hit it. The markers would be moving out of the government system and into the private sector and this needed to be taken into account. I had to develop a system where the government withdrawal and subsequent transfer could be hidden once the initial move was made. That would be a hard one, but I thought I could do it. So I was set.

I had the tag reader inner design layout, two different tag bracelets, the tag reader card, my own hideaway account, and the place and time of the move. That took me about ten weeks. The data layout of the

211

account was the most difficult, but I was able to hack the system and create the account. I made it appear as a charity account and tied it into the overall national charity system.

Charities are notorious for seeing their accounts jump and drop with significant amounts of funding moving through them at any given time. It was the nature of the beast. When they had a drive there was a spike and then that would be followed by a disbursement of funds.

In that system, charities were provided with formal accounting systems that maintained all their account transactions. The greatest part of this is they had security and anonymity. Not even the government interfered with the charity system. It gave me the perfect key to moving the markers around the country and sliding them off and into my own system. It was perfect.

All I needed was the transfer codes and indexing codes so that I could get the authorities to release the funds from the accounts. I needed to track their account activity and the only way I could do that was through the open tag reader line.

It took me a week to design and build the recorder device to be placed inside the tag reader while it was open for cooling. I needed two to three days of reading to get all the codes down right and once that was done then I was ready to program the transfer card and proceed with the job. I just needed the management at the station to stick with their current procedures and not get worried about what they were doing.

Now I needed to determine where I would hide the recorder and just how long it would take me to slide it into the tag reader. I figured I needed about ten seconds to do the job. I had worked on my activities at the station making sure I spent a lot of time on my hands and knees while tracing and photographing shadows and patterns off the floor. I had worked all over the station floor chasing shadow lines and layouts at all hours of the day to the point that the station workers got used to working around me.

Everything has gone so well and in just twelve short weeks at that. Now I was at a critical state, the planting of the transaction reader in the tag reader at the station. The emotions were off the charts. I kept thinking don't forget something now, not now. Bring the inert bracelet, the transaction reader, my camera and pads and pencils. Keep it normal, business as usual.

Pay no attention to the station workers, but keep an eye on them. If they follow their schedule they will be out of the station platform area within five to ten minutes after the last of the rush passes through.

I had selected the tag reader I wanted to bug and moved over to that side of the station to start my shadow chasing so that I could move in on the tag reader target.

As I entered the platform I almost lost my cool completely. There was a maintenance crew over by the target tag reader. At first I thought the game was over. I counted five technicians and the entire area within twenty feet of the reader was covered with canvas sheets and tools. I was screwed.

Cool down, relax and do your usual thing. Move over to the other side of the station platform and set to work. Wait, take some pictures of the technicians and their equipment and concentrate on the shadow effect that you have been working on all this time. In fact, I moved in close and even onto the canvas sheeting. I kept my attention on the shadow designs and incorporated the added design features of their equipment into my scheme.

It was a bold move, but it paid off. The head technician came over and looked at what I was doing and then asked me not to get too close to his crew. I asked how long they would be there and he advised just a cracked glass panel in the dome had to be replaced and they would be gone in about an hour.

My movements paid off. I was interested in the artistic elements of the domes patterns cast on the floor and this made me appear to be totally engrossed in the process of pursuing these patterns wherever they appeared. So I set to work and steered clear of the work crew and the tag reader line. They finished their job and cleared out and a cleanup crew moved in and cleaned up the mess they left behind.

Now I was alone and no more than three feet from the reader I had targeted. I slid my pattern frame across the floor so one corner was almost touching the tag reader and then moved around into a position where I could set my camera up and hide the tag reader with my body and I was set to install the tag reader scanner. One final breath and I slid the reader into the tag unit and popped it into place next to the sending unit.

It worked. No one came running and it was business as usual. It took everything I had to stay put and continue on with my shadow catching. I thought my usual ending time would never get there. I slowly moved back and away from the reader line and concentrated on another pattern that had just formed near the first bench I used when I first started this thing.

Just minutes before I was to stop and clear out the staff came through and started closing up the tag readers in preparation for the next commuter rush. As they moved closer to my bugged reader I felt myself tensing up. I watched the reader door close and the tech moved on to the next unit and that was that. My next big issue was recovering the bug in three days.

It was a killer time for me. I had to continue in my shadow chasing game and keep a low profile. Believe it or not the hardest part was keeping my attention away from the bugged reader. I just had to look over there every time someone went by it or walked close to it. My heart would stop when they would first open them in the morning and then come through a few hours later and close them. For three days it was like that.

Finally target day arrived. All I had to do was to recover the transaction reader and slip it into my case and move away from the target reader. I realized I had to keep my shadow chasing process as clean and normal as it has always been. No rushing right over to the target reader and no hanging around that location. I had to appear normal and random.

I knew I had about three hours to make the recovery and set my movements to that target. I wanted to be at the reader in two hours and make the recovery and then move on to my next photo layout. I had to make sure I made the bracelet change from my live bracelet to the inert one before I moved in on the reader and then get the normal bracelet back on immediately after I cleared the reader line.

At the one hour mark I was in position to make the recovery and had my camera and layout sheets in place. I looked at the dome and then moved around the layout sheets just as I had done a few hundred times in the past weeks. I was next to the reader when I looked up and to my horror there was a transit security officer standing just ten feet away from me and watching me.

I had no tag bracelet on and I was within three feet of the reader line and he had me cold. I looked at him and then over to the reader and then back to him and immediately moved over and away from the reader line. At the same time I was telling him I was sorry and almost begged him not to check me out.

He stood there watching me as I crawled away from the line and proclaimed my regrets and then he simply asked me if I ever sold any of my art. It stopped me short and I rose up on my knees, looked at him and told him yes that if I felt I got a good pattern and that it was crisp and clear I would put them up for sale. He nodded and said that he may contact me later about buying one and I told him any time and thanked him.

He then moved through the gate and disappeared down the walkway to the other side of the track and the far gate some two blocks away. I was shaking so bad I could hardly move let alone concentrate. But, I needed that recorder and then started to reposition myself by the reader. In less than two minutes I had the recorder in my case and my good tag bracelet back on and moving my equipment across the floor to another location. It took everything I had to stay in that station for the rest of my normal viewing period.

Finally it was time to pack up and start for the Fourth Street entrance. The crowds were already starting to enter the station and the techs were coming in behind me and closing up the tag readers. This platform was not open for service as yet, but there were numerous other platforms and the crowds were moving in those direction. In no time I was into and through the crowds and out onto Forth and heading home. It had been a most successful day.

The transaction recorder was crammed full of data. Three days of commuter information including all their tag readings and the data transfer transaction that followed. It was not hard to separate the tag reader transaction of the commuters from the banking transactions of the tag readers. Once I did that I needed to confirm the banking transaction numbers and make sure the sequencing was correct. That would take some time and it had to be right the first time I tested it. There was no room for error in this one.

Now I was ready. I had the transaction codes and they tested perfect. I was set to make the funds transfer from the Transit Authorities bank accounts into my own system. But, I would not be doing that from my home computer. My moves would leave a trail right back to my home computer and that would be the end of me.

No, I needed another location and it turned out to be another government computer that I would use. Every library had public access computers throughout the buildings. My next job was to find just the right one where I would have a degree of privacy and still be able to watch any and all activity around me. I needed one of the libraries on the other side of the city from where I lived and it had to be a fairly active location.

I had redesigned the tag reader recorder so that it was a two way recorder now and I needed to place that into the reader again. This unit would have to be reinstalled into one of the tag readers and would work as a network server as I connected to it from the library and then passed on into the tag reader and then into the Transit Authorities account system.

That meant two more trips to the tag reader, one to place the redesigned tag recorder and then one to retrieve it once the job was done. My time here would be critical. I would need to be at the library at the time the commuter crush was just ending and just before they opened the tag readers to cool them down. At that point I would start the transaction protocol and then close out of the library system and head back to the station to retrieve the tag reader.

It was a time critical situation and one that I needed to trust the fact that the employees at the station were used to me and would pay little or no attention to me and my usual activities. Next I needed to determine the day of the week I wanted to take action and I decided that a Friday was the best day. It was the end of the usually busy week and people were waiting for the day to end so they could go home for the weekend. It was the perfect day.

Don't ask me why, but I picked the next Friday the thirteenth for my move. Maybe it was a case of bravado or whatever. It just seemed appropriate for the activity I was about to get involved with. So, on the twelfth I was at the station at the usual time and usual place and started my shadow chasing. I worked my way to the tag reader line and successfully got the recorder/server unit installed in the same tag reader as before.

Friday morning I was at the library of choice at opening time and got to the computer I had selected and set to work. I had to make the connection between this computer and the recorder/server in the tag reader. At first I had a problem with getting through the library protocol, but with the help of one of the attendants was successful in making the connection.

Now I needed to install the transaction software into the tag recorder and set to work with that. I plugged my thumb drive into the terminal and entered my codes and the install took place. No problems or error. I now had thirty-five minutes to get across town and to the station at my regular time. By the time the commuter crowd had moved through the recorder/server would kick into gear and start the transaction system going.

I figured I would give it two hours of the three that the tag readers were open and then move in and recover the reader/server and leave. From then on the system would do the job and I could plan my move as need be.

I knew I would have to continue my presence in the station doing my shadow chasing so that I wouldn't bring undue concerns about me once the theft was discovered. If all went well I would leave nothing behind to tie me to it.

Traffic was a little congested this morning as I worked my way to the station. I was a few minutes late, but nothing that would give anyone reason to be concerned. All I had to do was play the game like I had set it up and make just one more move to the tag reader to remove the recorder/server from the machine and then I was free and clear, just that simple, that easy.

Why is it that after untold hours of planning and implementing a perfect plan that some unforeseen event enters in and just blows it all to hell? I mean it's like putting a puzzle together and then when you're placing the last piece in to place you accidentally hook the edge of the puzzle and dump the whole thing on the floor. It's just one of those little lapses in attention or whatever. And, I did it.

It was all perfect and all I had to do was recover the recorder/server. That was it, just one last little thing. I moved in on the machine and reached in and pulled the device out of the machine. It was done, all I had to do was move off across the floor and spend the rest of the day doing my thing. Then I simply reached out and closed the reader door. Why? Why the hell did I do that? What was I thinking? I closed that damn tag reader door and queered the whole thing.

I tried to stop it. I reached for it and just missed it by a fraction. And, it closed. I moved away from the machine as far as I could without being too obvious, but it was too late. I had only one option left and that was to get the hell out of there as fast as I could. I needed to dump the electronics I had built for this job someplace where they would never find them. I had but seconds and no more.

If they caught me they would kill me on the spot. No questions, no second chance, just a bullet through the head. I then saw the drain hole over by the pillar in the station floor. It was there so that when there were heavy rains water that came in through the doors and station platform, the rain water had a place to go. It was only ten feet away and I had to get the parts to it now. The reader/server and the inert bracelet had to go down that drain and now.

I pulled them both out and gave them a shove. They slid across the floor and the bracelet got there first and dropped into the drain. I could hear it falling and banging into the wall of the pipe on its way down to nowhere. The recorder/server started to slow down and seemed to be coming to a stop. It's only an inch or so to go and it was not going to make it. It was almost at a stop when it got to the drain opening and oh so slowly slipped over the edge and teetered in what seemed like hours and then dropped out of sight down the drain.

I heard the footsteps coming up behind me and then a body hitting me and knocking me flat. The wind went out of me and in short order I could feel myself floating upwards as someone grabbed me by the neck and jerked me to my feet.

All I could think to do was cry out, "I hit the door with my elbow. I did not mean to be that close to the machine. I was just concentrating on taking a picture and I moved around and hit the door of the machine with my elbow and it closed. I'm sorry I didn't mean to do that."

They read my bracelet and dumped everything out of my bags and went through it all. It was just drawing material and a couple of cameras. I looked up and saw the security officer from a few days ago walking up and asking what was going on. They advised him that I had been messing around one of the tag readers. He turned to me and asked what I had to say and I told him I was setting up a photo of a new design I had just identified and as I moved around to get a better angle and clear any shadows from the shot I hit the tag reader door and it went shut.

I knew I was too close, but the picture was just perfect and I was concentrating on that and not on where I was. I didn't mean to do it and wish to hell I hadn't.

He went over to the tag reader and opened it up and looked inside. Nothing, it was just a tag reader and nothing had been touched or moved inside the machine. He came back over to me and made sure I understood the seriousness of the situation. I told him that I was scared out of my mind and that I would never do that again. In fact I felt that maybe I had better look for some other location to continue my artistic endeavors. He agreed and advised me to end my presence at that location. I had just over stayed my welcome.

With that they released me and I quietly picked up all my tools and was escorted out of the station. As I walked away I turned and walked back to the security officer and handed him a photo slide and told him I wanted him to have one of my design pictures and that again I was really sorry for screwing up. He took the photo slide and thanked me and told me not to come back. I agreed and headed home.

The news hit the wires two days later. An undisclosed amount of funds had been removed from the Transit Authorities banking accounts and at that point had not been tracked or found.

A day later I had moved to a local park, again it was covered with a rather complex dome structure and I was busy tracking shadows and taking pictures. They pulled up in two cars and approached me. I did not really know they were there until one of them tapped me on the shoulder. As I looked up I saw the four of them in their uniforms and with rather stern looks on their faces.

As I stood up they checked my tag bracelet and then took my photo bag and started going through it. I asked what was going on and one of them looked at me and advised that they would ask the questions and not me.

He asked why I had no longer been coming to the station to do my shadow chasing and I told them what had happened and that I had been told never to return to the station again because I had gotten too close to the tag reader line and had hit one of the doors and caused it to close. In effect I had been thrown out of the place and planned never to go back. The look on his face told me he didn't believe me, so he called the station security unit and checked on my story.

Every now and then luck just has to get in on the act and for me it happened this time. Who else would come on the line than the very officer that had kicked me out of the station on that fateful day? He confirmed my story and also advised that the machine had checked out clean at the time and that he would enforce my ban if I ever showed up again.

With that the officers thanked me and left. There I was shaking like a bowl of Jell-O still not knowing if I had pulled it off or not. I needed to get to a library, not the one I had worked at, and check into my account to see if it had happened as I had planned. Yet, I

228

needed to stay put for a few days, actually another two weeks at the least.

I had to give them time to try and find the funds and then try and track the controller of those funds. So, I sat tight. I continued to go to the park and do my thing. Just being quiet and slowly and methodically tracking each shadow cast through the dome and taking my pictures. I am sure they were watching me and I needed to continue life as usual.

Then I had a thought. I can only chase shadows in this park so long before I needed to move on to something else. So, the day came when I made a change and it was an odd one at that. Instead of looking for more shadow locations I simply got up and walked across the street to the nearest building. Moved to the corner of that building and set my camera up and started looking at the details of the building itself. You, know. The texture, the materials, the colors and shading they used.

The particular building I picked was an older one with many ornate features. I started looking at the lines and layout of the structure and then started positioning my equipment to take the pictures. Sure enough here they came.

Two of them, dressed in the usual gray outfits. First of all, they walked by me taking in my equipment and the fact I was looking at the wall and not paying any attention to the world around me. Finally they approached me and asked what I was up to.

I went into the details of my project and how each stone, each line and curve, and the color of the structure presented unique design features that I felt would make for great photographs. I guess I was good at my job because in short order they became bored with me and moved on. I'm sure their report of my activities would end up in a file in some cabinet off in some corner in a basement.

Well there you have it. That was three years ago and I am now relaxing in a custom built mountain retreat and living the good life. The fact is my photography front had also worked out for me and I became quite famous for my structural and shadow pictures. I made a small fortune in that endeavor alone. But, my biggest fortune came by means of the tag readers.

Do you know how much funding is transferred during the rush hours at the transit stations in my home town? Well let's just say that I could spend a quarter of a million marks a day and still be earning interest that would far exceed the earnings of any of the upper level managers working for the authority.

Oh, the tag reader issues of leaving the units open after each rush hour ended. Within a month new readers were installed in all the stations throughout the metropolitan area. And, yes the station manager of the location of my activity was reassigned to another location. I never returned to that station. Even the thought of it was repulsive. Five to six months on my hands and knees crawling around on that floor tracking shadow lines was enough. Life is good, as they say…

Frank walked me to the back of the store and there on one of the shelves was the photo equipment that had been used by Steven. He looked at me. "Delbert, these items were used at a time after now, this time we're in. I have had them on that shelf for as long as I have been here, but in the future some time Steven came into the store and bought them and used them.

"Once he was done with them they returned to the shelf and are still there. Now the curious thing about those items and others that will be used in the future, we see them, you and I, there on the shelf. But anyone other than the person who is going to buy them cannot and never will see them. That Delbert is the nature of Duker's Store."

"Have I got you confused yet?"

I stood there looking at the shelf and then back over to where the flight helmet was hanging. "You're telling me that there are people across the spectrum of time who are coming into Duker's Store and buying items they need that will change their lives and many times the lives of those around them, is that right?"

"You've got it Delbert. In this job you will see items come and go and sometimes you will not know what is going on until that item returns and then the whole of that event is there for you to experience."

"What about the past, is the same thing happening there as well?"

"No, the past is the past and it becomes the past as that time moves by you. Anything that is in the past has been witnessed by you when they enter the store and purchase whatever is needed at that moment. The history of events remains as they are and you can go back and see them as they had happened in that past time. The difference between the past and the future is that the past can no long impact you. It already has while the future is in the process of impacting the time that will follow.

"No change will occur until your time reaches that point when the incident took place and then you will note the change."

This was getting more and more confusing all the time. Now the past was intermingling with the future and I was standing right between them. This management of the Duker's Store was getting to look more and more like a balancing act of major proportions.

Chapter Nine

Mark Norton

I had a feeling that my lessons were not over yet. Frank started to walk toward the rear door that went into the back of the store. I followed wondering just what was next in this amazing transformation I was going through.

As we got to the door he turned to me. "Now Delbert you need to prepare yourself for this next session. What you will witness next is something that cannot be. In fact it's impossible, but you must understand that it is real and it is as you will see it."

With that he turned, opened the door and stepped through then motioned for me to step through the door. When I did, the lights went on and there before me was a room so big that I could not see the end or either side from where I was standing. The ceiling itself had to be two hundred feet up.

I looked at Frank and then stepped further into the room and turned to him. "This is unreal. You're telling me that this room is actually here and I'm not hallucinating?"

"Delbert, this is the actual back room of Duker's Store. In this room you will find everything anyone on the face of the earth would want or come here to buy. I cannot tell you where each item is, but when a request is made for an item and you come back here to get it you will go directly to it and then deliver it to the customer.

"Don't ask me to explain it to you. In all the years I have been here I have never figured it out. All I know is that when an item is asked for it is here and it will find its way to you."

"But Frank, when I stand outside and look at the store there is nothing behind it this big. In fact if I were to walk around the whole of the store there would be nothing to indicate that there was a storage capability this big in this store. I guess what I'm saying is that nothing on the outside of the store gives any sign of a room this size inside of the store."

This was unreal and I could not come to fully understand what I was seeing or what Frank was saying. There are around seven to eight billion people on earth and there are items in this back room for every one of those seven or eight billion that may come to Duker's Store for whatever. There has to be a God after all.

"Delbert let me tell you of another individual who visited Duker's Store. His name was Mark Norton and his story is as unreal as they come yet it happened. He came here for some highly specialized equipment that he would need in his coming situation.

...It's a part of your life. You hardly ever think about it and seldom really consider its benefits. Yet without it we cannot survive anywhere. The human Id is tied to it and can no more live without it than any other necessity in life.

But, when you're denied it, it becomes the focal point of your conscience and soul. Just the idea of the warmth that washes across your body as the light of it hits you. Even in the coldest of places, when it lands on you even the cold seems to diminish.

So, finding yourself down in a hole fifteen to sixteen thousand feet deep really separates you from the warmth and brightness of the suns light. Down there it's black as black. When the lights go out the blackness closes in on you and there is no sense of standing, sitting, or falling, it's a total envelopment, and a strait jacket of darkness. Even sound seems to fall short of reaching out.

The blackness can be so complete that when it hits it feels like a physical impact. It jars your body, your mind with its suddenness. At that point even food and water become secondary to you finding light, any light.

I have crawled around and through many caves, tunnels and mine shafts, but this one was a new experience. I guess the real fear that I feel is the fact I know little if anything about this place. I know that it was once a deep shaft mining system, I believe gold or some other precious metal of that nature. I guess it had been closed now for some fifteen years or so. It had been well kept and its mechanical features were still operating well. Yet, that did not compensate for the situation I now found myself in.

Three weeks ago I was contacted by the geological survey company that had been hired to evaluate the mine for future activation. My name is Mark Norton and I am an expert in deep mine management. This time they were looking for a new substance that only just became a valued market commodity. It was called Zurlium, a strange substance that had both metal and glass qualities. That is, it was a metal but it appeared to be made of glass or a glass like substance.

In its raw form it was brittle and a bugger to work with, but once successfully processed it was light, strong, and clear as water. It was perfect for deep water application and even more valued for deep space usage. Imagine a window made of metal that had the strength and weight properties of tungsten, perfect for deep space expeditions and probes.

It was my job, with the aid of three other individuals to carry out an on the scene exploration of the deep shaft mine to determine the location of any Zurlium and to take measurement for the purpose of determining the volume of Zurlium that was present in the mine. It should have been a one day job, but things have a habit of getting more complicated for me from time to time, and this was one of those times.

Upon taking the job offer I immediately went into town and found a hardware store that I felt would carry the equipment I needed for this job. One particular item was an Oxygen Meter, a device that would keep track of the Oxygen levels in the mine while we were down there carrying out the survey.

Along with that, I would like a system or meter that could measure the humidity as well and temperature and pressures at that depth.

I had gone to the store and found a single parking stall in front of the place. I had parked and went in. As I closed the door behind me I turned and there was a man standing there with this really odd smile on his face. "Welcome to Duker's Store, what can I provide for you?" He said.

I can tell you one thing, in the thirty seconds I stood there looking at him and the insides of that store I thought if anyplace had an Environmental Monitoring Meter or System, this was the place. Sure enough he had one and oddly enough it was sitting on the counter just five feet from me, almost as if it had been waiting there for me.

Well I bought the meter and left the store, returned to the motel and started to pack my back pack for the next day's trip down into the mine. I was excited about the job and ready to take it on.

I had with me three experts in the prospecting of Zurlium. Dave, that is Dave Dundee, was the lead prospector. He had somewhere around fifteen years in the business and was known for finding the largest vein of Zurlium ever found. Steven Anders was his second hand in the business and had almost as many years of experience as Dave. Tad Russell was the geologist who was there to confirm our findings.

We came down the shaft fully equipped with all the lighting and food and survival needs for an expedition of one day. We had not anticipated that it would have been any longer. It was going well and we had found rich veins of the mineral in several locations and only had three locations left to do when things went south on us.

Deep mines like this one are accidents waiting to happen. Whether anyone was there or not, they happened. In this case we were there when all hell broke loose. It started with an earth quake. Down here they are common and in short order you get used to them. So, when this one hit it was not anything out of the ordinary. It became out of the ordinary in a fraction of a second after it started.

We were probably four hundred fifty feet from the main shaft when it hit. Dave stopped short and looked at me. "That doesn't sound right."

He no sooner got the words out when a slab of the ceiling of the tunnel between us and the main shaft dropped. I have no idea how thick in a horizontal direction it was. All I know is that the whole of the roof dropped in one solid mass, almost as if a giant had stomped his foot down on the ground above and that drove the slab straight down onto the tunnel floor.

It was solid, not a slide of broken up rocks and dust. It was more like a door slamming shut, a solid rock door. Without a doubt we were not going to dig our way through it. Tad approached the wall and determined that our first impressions were right. We would not be going out that way.

I had had the opportunity to look over the layout of the mine before we descended and had a detailed map of the mine with me. That was going to be our only salvation. Was there a way out of this tunnel and back to the main shaft?

Steven was the first to recommend that we conserve our batteries so that we could extend their time. So, we started to use only one of the four lamps we had at a time. We had one back up battery for each one. Each battery was good for six to seven hours of continuous running. With eight batteries that gave us forty to fifty-six hours of light.

Our next concern was food and water. We had only brought enough for the day so we had to combine and conserve all the food supplies. Water was another story. That was in short supply and the ground water in the mine was questionable. We had to find it first and then determine whether we could use it or not.

Once we were organized we decided it was time to move out. There was only one direction we could go and that was away from the fall and the main shaft. Further into the deep shaft mine and further into the unknown. I pulled out the Oxygen meter and checked the current level, they were within acceptable levels.

By the map the shaft we were in was somewhere around two miles long. It indicated that there were three shafts that branched off of this main shaft. Two indicated dead ends but the third indicated 'extended', whatever that meant.

One thing was certain and that was the fact that those above, on the surface, where not going to dig us out any time soon. That is if they knew there had been a cave in. We didn't even know if they could get down into the mine let alone work on the slide area.

Also, there was no way they would be drilling a new shaft down to us any time soon. A shaft fifteen to sixteen thousand feet deep would take weeks if not months to accomplish.

If a search party did respond, they had no idea where we were. We were in this thing on our own. Then Dave said out loud what the rest of us were thinking. "If they missed us and find the slide, they can make a good guess that we are on the other side of the slide somewhere. The question is how thick was the slide? There was no way for us to know."

So off we went into the unknown hoping that we would find some way out going this direction. It was better than sitting there and wondering as to whether they will ever find us or even try looking for that matter.

Being this deep into the earth's crust is interesting, to say the least. First of all is the heat. Up toward the surface, when you start into the ground, you will find that the temperature of most caves is a constant forty-five degrees. But once you pass the five thousand foot mark there is a noted change in the ground temperature. It has to be around one hundred ten degree right now.

Next is the darkness of any area outside of our light. Just a small indentation in the wall is so dark there is no sense of texture or feature to the wall. It's just black.

Sound, there is no echo of any kind. In fact it's a flat dead sound. As you speak the sound of your voice seems to drop straight to the floor. If you clang something it's just a dull clank with no reverberation or anything. Yet, even a whisper can be heard some twenty to thirty feet away.

As a matter of fact, all your senses are subdued. That is, you feel compressed, enclosed. It's hard to describe, but you feel all alone even when there are three other people with you.

We finally came to tunnel three. It was located almost half way between tunnels one and two which exited this main shaft to the right while tunnel three exited to the left. It was about this time that we began to hear something. It's almost indescribable, yet it was clearly there, somewhere behind us and off into that dead blackness beyond our light.

We stood silent for maybe ten minutes listening for that sound, but there was nothing. It was a low raspy sound, one that comes from deep down inside. Yet it was so quiet and still. We were sure we heard it, but could not determine if it was the ground around us settling or if it came from something that was alive. It made the hair on my neck stand up.

After we had moved down tunnel three about two hundred yards we came to a fork which was not indicated on the map we had and we had no idea which was the main tunnel or shaft and which was not. They both appeared to be the same size as far as diameter was concerned and they appeared to be about the same age.

We had to make a determination as to which one to take, but we also needed to make sure that we did not get lost. We needed to mark this location in the event we ended up coming back through the other tunnel. Steven picked up a number of rocks and placed them to the far side of the opening of the tunnel on the left and we then set out to the right.

It was about this time that I had that feeling of being watched come over me. I don't know what it was but, I had a feeling that someone or something is close by and watching our every move. Yet there was no sound, nothing that would indicate that there was anything there or nearby. It's that creepy crawly feeling that one gets from time to time.

It was Tad that first noticed it. He started taking close up looks at the tunnel walls and running his hands over them. At first I thought that he found a Zurlium vein, but then he did something curious. He leaned forward and sniffed the wall. That stopped all of us. "What the hell are you doing?" I asked.

He held up his hand in a jester that told me to hold on. By this time we all had come to a standstill.

Tad then turned. "Tunnel walls this deep and far from the surface are not

246

supposed to have animal blood on them, but these do."

Steven walked over to the wall and sniffed it and then stepped back and looked at Tad, and then he turned to Dave and me and nodded.

"Not possible." I said. "That is simply not possible. No animal could live down here let alone have another one present that could and would kill it. Besides that, there are no bones or hair anywhere around here that would support this."

Tad stood there looking at me. "Listen, I agree that is highly unlikely, but I have been a hunter for most of my life and I know an animal kill when I find one. That is blood on that wall and it's not been there that long."

I again had that strange feeling of being watched only this time it was more acute considering what we had just found.

"Guys, I think we need to keep moving. I don't like what we have found and we need to locate a way out of here as fast as we can. I have a feeling we don't want to be here any longer than necessary. There is something going on here that I cannot put my finger on, but I feel as if we need to move and move fast." I picked up my lamp and started walking on down the tunnel.

Tad came around me and took the lead and we started further down the tunnel. Steven followed up and kept talking so that we would not lose contact with him. With only one light being used that meant that Tad had it at the front of the line and Steven had to walk in the near dark behind us. Dave was between Steven and me. We kept a continuous conversation going in order to keep tabs on each other and for the fact that we felt better hearing each other talking.

We had gone maybe another hundred yards when I asked Steven a question and there was no answer. There was dead silence, not a sound. Tad stopped and Dave and I turned to see why Steven had not answered and he was gone. There was nothing there. We moved back down the tunnel about thirty feet and still nothing. Not a mark on the floor or walls of the tunnel. Not a sound of any kind.

He was gone, almost like he had never been there. To make matters worse all his equipment had gone with him, the light and extra food and tools that we would need. Tad moved out into the darkness another twenty feet checking the ground and walls closely for anything that would tell us what the hell was going on. Ten feet further we found Steven's jacket, backpack and supplies lying on the floor of the tunnel.

The sleeves of his jacket were split from cuff to shoulder and across his chest to the zipper. The jacket had literally been sliced from his body, yet there was not a sign of blood or anything. What could do that? What was so fast and so powerful that a man could not even get a sound out when it hit him? What could slice his jacket with such precision that not even a drop of blood was left and yet cut the material cleanly?

Panic set in. We had just had one of our team separated from us so fast and so completely that there was not even time to react. We started to run and there was only one direction to go and that was deeper into the tunnel and away from the scene of this happening.

It may have been five minutes later that we finally stopped running because we were physically exhausted. We had to think this thing out and set up some kind of a defense against whatever it was that we were dealing with. Steven was gone and we were sure that he would never be coming back. There was a predator in the tunnel with us and it was fast and powerful. We needed to develop a plan and strategy to deal with it.

Unfortunately one of the strategies was the need to use more than one of the lights at the same time. We needed light in front of us and light behind us. We also needed to keep a continuous watch in both directions. If there was something behind us we had to assume that some kind of animal was in fact living in this mine and that it or others could be in front of us as well.

Tad started thinking out loud about this creature and what it had to be. "The first thing is that it had to be of a significant size and well-muscled. This made it fast and powerful. Next, if it was of any considerable size then that meant there had to be a supply of game for it to harvest and feed on. There had to be a food chain involved. Nothing could live down here without there being a continuous supply of food."

If true, then that meant we were clearly not alone down here and that we had a major problem. Some predator had discovered us and it was now stalking us as its prey. In addition, there had to be a labyrinth of tunnels and caves in this area. This wildlife could not survive in just the manmade tunnels down here. Logic took us one step further. If there is a labyrinth of tunnels there may well be a number of ways up and out of this place.

Seventy five feet further down the tunnel we found a break in the tunnel wall. It was about eighteen inches wide and cut clear up through the ceiling of the tunnel and out of sight. Just then Tad heard it again, that low raspy sound that we thought we heard before but could not pin down. The only difference was that it was clearer and it was coming from down the tunnel behind us.

Dave stepped into the cut and shined his lamp down into the cut and saw that it dead ended about twenty feet back. There were a large number of rocks laying around on the floor and piled up against the wall. You could see where the pile had fallen from.

We had moved back into the cut and then it hit. We were too far in the cut for it to reach us, but it sure as hell tried. It lunged at the cut and reached in as far as it could. We managed to get a light on it and all we could see was this massive paw that had to be at least sixteen inches across. The claws were as massive, around twelve inches long. No wonder we had not heard Steven make a single sound. When paws that size hit you there is such power behind it that you would not even feel it hit. It was probably over so quick that he never had a chance to think.

Now it had us pinned. We were trapped in the cut and the only apparent exit was blocked by something beyond description. Our choices were limited, stay there and die of starvation or lack of water or try to fight our way past this thing and end up being cut in half, great choices.

We knew one thing, and that was that this creature was not going to stop. After trying unsuccessfully to reach us it started to dig. In about five minutes it has carved out a six foot hole into the cut and was making head way. We had just minutes to decide what to do and it would be on top of us.

About this time Tad's light gave out. We had what was left of Dave's and mine and the recovered light of Steven's that was partially used up. We also had four batteries. Tad removed and replaced his battery and meanwhile I turned on mine to keep the creature illuminated while we tried to work ourselves out of this dilemma.

As best as I could tell from my position, this animal was like nothing I had ever seen before. When you looked beyond his paw, you could see its face. It appeared to be a rather squat animal. That is, it had short wide set legs and its body was broad and appeared to be very dense. Its head was also wide and narrow from the bottom or chin to the top of its head.

If I were to match its general features with any animal, I knew I would say it appeared somewhat like a badger in general build and shape, except it was at least four times larger than the largest badger around.

Needless to say, it appeared to be extremely powerful and a man would never stand a chance against it.

Meanwhile, Dave had started to look beyond our position in the cut. He had found an area where he could climb up the face of the cut. As he climbed it became easier for him to find hand holds and in fact the cut seemed to lean away from us, meaning that it was more like crawling across the face of the cut than up it. As he approached the top of the tunnel that was level with the cut he called back and told us that the cut was opening up and spreading out. With that Tad and I started after him. I was glad to leave that animal behind us.

In about ten minutes we found ourselves standing in a low ceiling room about fifteen by fifteen feet in size. Dave pulled out a pack of matches and lit one. As we watched the flame we noted that it was being blown away from the cut and off to our right to a hole in the wall of the room. As we moved to the hole you could feel the air flowing past you as it left the room and entered the hole.

It was obvious that there was a way out of this area and that the air was moving toward an opening or maybe a larger room. We had no choice but to follow that air wherever it went. We were leaving the known areas of the mine and heading into the unknown. We were around three miles down and venturing into areas where no human being had ever ventured before.

Besides that, the mega badger was still back there digging and driving into the cut with everything it had. It was obvious that this thing was not going to stop and that we had maybe an hour's head start on it before it got to this room. When it did we did not want to be here.

If there were predators like the one we left behind down here, then who knows what else could be down here. At that point I did not give us much chance of surviving this situation. The odds were against us in the extreme.

Dave was either losing his mind or he had more damn guts than I had ever imagined. He stormed through the tunnel like a mad man, every five to ten feet he would let out a yell that at first I was sure that he had just ran into another creature or something. But he had not and he drove himself ahead yelling all the way. In time all three of us were yelling and making as much noise as we could.

Dave had employed the old concept, when in bear countries make lots of noise so that you do not surprise a bear. The theory being that any bears would be more afraid of you than you are of them, and it gave them the chance to get out of our way. Whether it worked or not I don't know. I never ran around in bear country, so who knows. Anyway, it was better than nothing. Besides we kept in touch that way.

After about ten minutes of crawling on our hands and knees I was about done in, but, Dave kept driving ahead nonstop. He was like a man possessed. It made no difference whether we had a place or destination he was just driving ahead.

I almost ran head long into Tad's butt. Dave had come to a dead stop, still talking, but with a high level of excitement in his voice. Tad was trying to get a view around him, but all he had in front of him was Dave's butt. Finally Dave dropped to his stomach and twisted around and yelled back at us. "It's an opening." He said. "Move easy and slowly."

With that he moved ahead and disappeared from sight. Shortly Tad did the same and then I came to the opening, finding Dave and Tad sitting on the ground looking straight ahead. The opening dropped almost straight down and from my position I could not see what they were looking at. They sat there motionless. I moved ahead and down onto the ground beside Dave and managed to get myself swung around and into a sitting position when I saw it.

The only way I can describe it is that we were sitting in the mouth of a cave looking out over a valley. How else could I say it? That was a valley out there in front of us. It stretched off into the distance on all sides of the panorama that we could see from the caves mouth.

Dave seemed to twitch. He sat there and twitched, like a person who was seeing something that could not be. That was impossible to be, but yet there it was. There were no plants, just sand, dirt, rocks and a stream running through it. The formations scattered across the landscape were of stalagmites and stalactites that had come together forming huge columns and reaching up beyond our view of the cave entrance.

We're three miles down in the crust of the earth with no sunlight anywhere. Sunlight, what the hell! There's sunlight out there. It seemed to hit all three of us at the same time. We could see way out into the valley and it was light. The impact was huge.

What the hell had we gotten ourselves into anyway? This was simply impossible. Dave moved forward to the edge of the cave mouth and looked up. What first appeared as a valley was actually a huge cavern. The ceiling of this place was way and to hell above us. There had to be several hundred feet to even a thousand feet to the ceiling of this cavern. The ground tapered off from the mouth of the cave down to the floor of the cavern another two or three hundred feet down the slope.

I could see the walls of the cavern running away from the caves mouth in both directions, but I could not see the other side of the valley. It was enormous. There is no other way to describe it. Yet, it was there with three miles of earth sitting on top of it, it was there right in front of us.

The next thing we noticed was that there were dust storms moving across the floor of the cavern. We could feel the wind against our face. Some of it was coming from back in the cave, but most of it was from within the cavern. Were there other ways in and out of this place?

But the light, where was it coming from, how can it be? It should be total darkness, black, lightless. But, it was there bright and shiny. There were shadows from the structures and alongside the rocks. By the position of the shadows we could tell where the light was coming from and it was to our left and far down the valley. The decision had been made for us. We had to go to the light.

The question now was by which route. We could stay up on the edge of the valley and follow the wall around to the source. Or, we could take the direct route down by the stream and directly to the light source. We had to take into consideration the wildlife that was probably present because of the mega badger we had left behind in the tunnel. We checked our water supply and decided to replenish it and then take the upper route around the wall.

As we started down toward the stream, Tad noticed a small dust storm moving down the other side of the stream coming toward us. He took notice of it because of the size and that it appeared to be going against the wind. Within seconds we could see that it was not a dust storm, but a small herd of animals moving along the bank of the stream.

They were a strange looking creature. Again they had the squat legs similar to that of the mega badger, but that ended the similarity. Their bodies were rounder and higher than that of the badger. I would say they were maybe half again the badger's size and appeared to be heavier as well. Their heads were again, rounded with extremely large eyes. Their mouths were more pig shaped and oversized for the size of their head. It was obvious that they root for food and were not meat eaters, which would prove to be a wrong assumption. It appeared that there were twenty-five to thirty of them in the herd.

As they moved along the bank we noted that two or three of them were posted out away from the main body. In all probability they were scouts or lookouts, something like that. Tad then noticed that beyond them there was movement.

We had to stop and look hard to see them, two mega badgers just over the dune that ran parallel to the stream. It was clear they were stalking the herd. Dave noted that they hunted in teams and that we must have been faced with two of them back in the mine unless one of them had been killed in the slide.

We stayed among the rocks as we watched the mega badgers working their way into position for the best attack on the herd. My first thought was that this was going to be a pig shoot. The herd animals had no way of repelling or resisting the attack of these two monsters. What I did not pay attention to was the fact that the badgers were being so careful.

It dawned on Tad that they were not just diving into the herd. They were working themselves around into an attack position, but one that could give them the best chance of cutting just one of the herd members out of the group. The question was why? They had the size and muscle to literally move in and take anyone they wanted and then carry it away. The herd could do nothing about it.

What happened next was beyond anything we could ever imagine let alone anticipate. What we had forgotten was that in this terrain there appeared to be no vegetation. No grass, brush, trees, moss, nothing that resembled plant life.

Then what did the herd eat? They appeared to be rooting type animals and our assumption there was right except that they were rooting for living ground dwellers and not plants. We were about to find out why the badgers were being so careful.

The badgers moved into a position of best advantage. As the herd moved by the larger of the two started the attack. They had selected what appeared to be an older member of the herd that was at the back of the herd and furthest away from the stream. As soon as the badger attacked the three guards immediately moved toward the badgers.

This was different. Normally herd animals would call out a warning and everyone would stampede away from the danger. It was everyone for their selves. This was not the case. They in fact turned and attacked toward the advancing badgers. The first guard moved between the badger and the target animal and went up on it hind legs. Holding its hoofs out in front of itself it then unsheathed a set of claws like none I had ever seen before.

The badger reacted immediately by breaking and bearing off and away from the guard animal. The second badger took up a defensive position giving the attacking badger the time he needed to retreat from the threat. In just seconds the predatory badger was now the prey as the herd guards and the rest of the herd reacted to the attack. Stalemate, the badgers backed off but now had taken up a defensive position at the top of the dune.

It became clear that this environment was not that of a predator/prey system, but, was instead a predatory system where all the creatures that lived here were in fact predators. That, my friend put us right in the middle of a serious situation. We now knew that we had to keep out of sight and out of the way of any of the animals that inhabit this place. Everything was going to be a meat eater and we were now a target.

Thirty minutes later we had our water and were walking along the upper wall of the cavern. The route was not difficult and there appeared to be animal trails all along this area. We also noted that the walls were pock marked with caves and indentations that could be the burrows for some kind of animal. We would have to be careful to make sure we were not walking into a trap.

We may have gone a hundred feet when Tad found a weapon. Well, not actually a weapon, but one that could be used as a weapon. It was a stick of rock about five feet long and came to a point on both ends. It would make a perfect spear. Within twenty minutes we had found two more and were now fully armed for our journey. We managed to find several clubs along the way as well.

Twenty minutes later we saw a rock spear sticking up out of the ground. As we approached the spear we noted that it was sticking through the skeleton of an animal. It had been there for some time.

At first we thought that maybe there were humanoids in the cavern, but after looking at the skeleton and then noting a number of broken spear rock lying around that area we determined that they were fall rocks from the ceiling of the cavern. That was the only thing they could be. That felt great thinking that we could get killed that way as well.

Two hours into the trek we could see the far end of the cavern. The light source was strong there and we also noted that the heat was increasing as we moved in that direction. We had seen a number of animals down by the stream, after the earlier contact, none of which appeared to be a problem for us at that point. We were particularly concerned about the mega badger showing up. It dawned on us that particular creature may well be trapped back in the tunnel as a result of the cave in, but there could be and probably were many others.

We finally reached the limits of our endurance and had to stop for a while and regain our strength. We ate our rations and then settle down for a rest. Dave took first watch and we figured we would get a few hours of sleep each and then move on.

Six hours later we were on the trail again. We had heard a number of animal cries during our down time and had seen a fairly large herd of animals, the likes of which we had never seen before. Not anything like the badger or herd before. We headed out with our goal being the light source.

As we approached the end of the cavern we saw a lake that stretched out across the width of the cavern and was maybe a quarter mile from the end of the cavern. At that point we saw the source. It was a round spot of intense white light in the wall of the cavern to the right side of the lake and about a hundred feet above the surface of the lake. We were on the left side of the lake and so decided to work our way around from that side and above the lake.

The heat in that area was considerable, we could tell that the lake may be hot, but it was not boiling. Three hours later we were nearing the light source. Well, getting as close as we were going to get. From that position I could tell that the light was in fact round and about two hundred fifty feet in diameter. As we looked at the source we could see that there was a lens over the face of the opening.

Behind it was clearly a swirling mass of superheated lava.

It hit me that there was nothing on this earth that could withstand that hot a temperature and still remain solid, except for Zurlium. We were looking at a natural formation of Zurlium. The earth had processed it and produced a clear lens that held the superheated lava back and this became the light source for the cavern. The entire environment of this location was dependent on that Zurlium lens and its ability to withstand the heat.

As we took a more in-depth look at the setup we learned that the whole wall of the cavern in that area was made up of Zurlium and when the heat of the earth's core hit the raw metal ore it processed it into the transparent form that we were working to achieve.

Tad had been looking at the rock formations and noted that some of the rock that reached down into the lake was actually causing the water to steam up and as the steam moved up into the air we could see it swirling around and forming into a column and rising up and into a large crack in the upper side of the cavern. At that point it seemed to pick up speed and dive into the crack and disappear.

Tad was staring at that crack. "I wonder."

I looked over at him. "What's going on?"

He looked at me. "I think that we have just found the way out of this mess for us."

I looked at the crack and the water steam going into it. "Is that the way out?"

Tad nodded his head.

We replenished our water supply and then moved out for the crack. The crack ran diagonally across the face of the wall, starting on our left, not more than a half mile from where we were standing and then angling up to the right across the top of the Zurlium wall and then off into the distance of the cavern ceiling.

The prospect of crossing over the top of that Zurlium lens did not sit well with me, but the only other way out of this place was crossing the valley floor and then the stream and then climbing the vertical cliffs on the other side to reach the crack. We had little choice.

When we got to the crack it was almost like climbing stair steps. The grade was bearable and by this time we would have put up with anything to get out of there. Three hours later we found the portal. We could feel the wind blowing past us and the water vapor that was in it. The heat was not unbearable and so we entered.

I stopped for a few minutes and looked back on the cavern and the situation we had come through. I knew we had a long way to go, but we had made it this far and we would make it the rest of the way. My mind went to Steven and the close call we had had with that animal way off in the distance. I would be glad to be out of this place.

Three miles straight up is one hell of a climb. The shaft we were working our way through was not overly large and in some places it was downright narrow. Yet it gave us ample hand and foot positions for climbing. We still had the issue of animals that may be in hiding as we climb. Dave took his spear with him and I kept my club.

As we climbed I thought about the adventure we had just been on. We have been gone just short of a week now and have managed to survive, although it's been rough, and we lost Steven. We had proven that there was Zurlium down there and that it could be used for high heat applications. I hope we can return to this place and kept telling myself that we must mark the entrance when we get to the top.

After a seemingly endless climb we reached the entrance. We could feel the change in temperature as we climbed the last five thousand feet. When we stepped out into the open we found ourselves on the side of a bluff overlooking the main mining facility. We weren't more than three hundred yards from the office.

Three months later a full discovery team descended into the shaft heading for the cavern below. The team consisted of twenty-five people ranging from professional hunters to the finest of geologists, anthropologist and the rest of the modern sciences. The target was a complete exploration of the cavern and surrounding caves in the search for the Zurlium and in studying the Zurlium lens that held the superheated lava back.

Me? I decided that I wanted to spend a few years on the beach by the ocean and away from anything that even suggested going down or into the ground in any way. I had no desire to revisit that place and in particular I had no desire having the possibility that I may meet up with the mega badger. I took my pay and retired for a while.

Dave and Tad went back with the expedition in hopes of finding the main Zurlium vein and in cataloging the different animal species that lived within that cavern and region. Good luck to them.

I was far more appreciative of the sun and its life giving light after that. I found it hard to get through the dark of the nights and always dreamed of the badger lurking in the shadows of the dark. For me sunlight was my life and my security. There was nothing there that could hide in the light. In the dark, everywhere was a hiding place. Can you hear that deep rustling sound, you know low, quiet, and deadly…

I looked at Frank knowing that the lessons I was learning were for my own good. The fact that an adventure as terrifying as this one must have been was disturbing to me, but one thing stood out.

"Frank, there is no metal known by the name of Zurlium. That tells me that there is something wrong. I guess it makes me think that not all of these stories are or were true. What do you have to say about that?"

He was smiling as I expressed my doubts about what was going on here. "Delbert, that is why I feel so sure that you are a special person and perfect for this job, I can understand that you doubt me and what I have said. But, I can assure you that this is fact and actually happened. Remember there is no time continuum here in this place. People will come here from all segments of the continuum both from the past, the present, and the future.

"Delbert, it's an issue of needs, needs of a person no matter where in the continuum they come from. Remember that Duker's Store is here on this street at this time, but it is also there in all the other times across the continuum.

"It's not an issue of whether Zurlium actually exists or not. Here in this time it does not and I agree with your observations. But Zurlium does exist in the future, in a time zone separate from this one. Remember, you walked into this store and when you did it was in your time zone, your part of the continuum. Everything we looked at is from that position, so some are from the present and some are from the future.

271

"Once you take the next step and assume my position here in the store there will be no specific time on the continuum for you. From there on when a need enters the store you will be there whether today, or a hundred years from now.

"Now let's move along and take another look at someone's experience with Duker's Store.

Chapter Ten

Stanley Delgodo

"Delbert, this situation is something that is entirely different from the others I have told you about, it is a future event from this point.

"This is about a man named Stanley that came to Duker's Store looking for the intangible. That element of one's life that is outside their experience and knowledge, the greatest issue is his relationship with his father and the events that were going to impact him.

"Know this, life can be dangerous and in this case this man must face an adversary that he never expected. He didn't know it at the time but what he needed was sitting here waiting for him to come and purchase it. There on that shelf is an RF Detector. That little box gives one the ability to check for audio surveillance bugs or hidden microphones.

Stanley didn't know it at the time and really didn't want to buy it, but when he saw it he knew that he would need it. He picked it up and then asked, "How much?"

I was pleased with his choice and smiled and advised him that it was just two hundred fifty dollars. He looked at it and then back to me. "That seems to be a little steep don't you think?"

I continued to smile and took the device and held it up in front of him. "Not if it saves your life."

He paid the price and then walked over to the door. He stopped and looked back at me as if he was going to say something and then turned and walked out the door.

…What a hammer head, this guy couldn't do anything without hurting himself in some way, shape, or form. Today was no different. Kelly Jennings was one of those people who simply survived. His entire life was spent putting himself back together again. Broken arms, legs, sprains, concussions, and just about anything one person could do to himself. No, he has not changed and that was going to be the main reason for the adventure we were about to be forced into.

I had not heard from Kelly in probably eight or maybe nine years, and my life had been better for it. I'm Stan that is Stanley Delgodo of the Harper Beach Delgodo's. My dad was worth more money than anyone person had a right to possess and he possessed it with gusto. That is, he possessed, and no one else in the rest of the family got anywhere near us, Dad's family. Dad doled it out like water being given to someone dying of thirst.

Did I love my dad? Well about as much as fifty bucks to buy next week's booze. We were all that way. His greed was something that each of us inherited. It was the one gift that he gave to us willingly. So I worked for a living until I was well set and seldom saw or approached my father unless it was to placate my mother. I guess, in a word I really hated his guts. Ah, the modern urban family in the whole.

Anyway, Kelly, for whatever reason, called one warm summer evening. I answered the phone and there he was. "Hi Stan."

It kind of set me back. Yes, I knew immediately who it was, what bothered me was why he would be calling me. "Kelly, what the hell's up?"

He paused, I guess for dramatic effect. "Stan, I've got a problem and when I ran into it I thought of you. Do you have five or ten minutes?"

With Kelly, whenever he approached you for anything the red flags flew at gale force. "Sure Kelly, what have you got?"

Again there was that dramatic pause. "Stan my man, I have got the key to a life time of fun and relaxation. But, I need a rich guy like you to get this thing moving."

The red flag pole had just broken off. "Wait Kelly, are you calling me for money?"

This time he came at me like a shark goes for a free meal. "Well, yes and no. I'm calling you because you have access to money and with that access we will be able to help each other out to the point of total independent wealth."

That rang a bell for me and I was hooked. "OK, Kelly what have you got?"

You could hear the triumph in his voice as he continued. "Not on the phone. I'll be there in Harper Beach in a week and I would love to get together with you and talk about this idea of mine and see if it really is something you're interested in."

I agreed to meet Kelly on Thursday, a week from tomorrow. With that Kelly told me he could not talk any longer and when he saw me he would fill me in on everything.

He tended to get overly dramatic when he is working one of his schemes. He was just that way, he telegraphed everything he was doing and as a result anyone who had any amount of money knowledge knew right off the bat that Kelly was up to something. Usually something no good or too costly to the person he has selected to benefit from his ideas.

That was a week ago and I find myself driving into town to the Harper Beach Royal Country Club to meet with Kelly in his room. As I parked my car I could not help but wonder what he was about to get me into and knowing his knack for self-mutilation I was a little more than concerned. But, my interest was pricked and I had to go.

It was a typical Kelly event, one of the best rooms in the hotel and of course all the best food. If Kelly was in need of money he sure did not show it. As I stepped into the room Kelly shook my hand. He had put on weight in the past eight or nine years. His hair was graying and thinning.

Kelly, when I last saw him, was a strong guy standing about six feet one and weighing in at around one hundred and ninety-five pounds. Today he was probably under six feet and was somewhere around two hundred and fifty. He looked a little worn and beat up, but he was Kelly through and through.

As I stepped into the room and closed the door Kelly moved ahead of me and promptly stumbled over the end of the bed. Yep that was Kelly Jennings in the flesh.

I knew one thing and that was I had to keep him focused and orientated to the topic at hand. He would take off on a tangent almost any moment and it took hours to get the real story out of him. "OK Kelly let's hear about it."

He held his hands up and motioned me to sit down. "In due time Stan, in due time. First I have some questions to ask you."

278

My guard went up immediately. This had not been in the original agreement and I told him so.

He was nodding his head and still waving his hands in front of me. "Relax I just need to know a few things."

I sat back, looking him in the eyes and trying to gauge his demeanor and any hidden agendas that may come popping up at any moment. "OK ask your questions."

He settled into the chair across from me and leaned forward, putting his forearms on his knees. "Your still married to that sweet girl you went to school with?"

Question one and what the hell did it have to do with this meeting. I answered him anyway. "Yeah, Kelly I am, except she lives in Chicago and I live here in Harper Beach."

A surprised look came across his face. "How long has that been going on?"

This was going to be boring as hell. "About seven years now."

He shrugged his shoulders. "Why don't you two get a divorce?"

What the hell did this have to do with anything and I was starting to get irritated. "Because we don't believe in divorce, that's why."

Kelly waved his hands again. "What do you do for women then?"

Now he was getting more than personal and it was really pissing me off. "I don't and if I did I would not tell you."

Kelly got this innocent look on his face. "Gees Stan, calm down and pull in your horns."

Now I was shaking my head and looking him square in the eyes and driving home my feelings. "Well Kelly, there are things you don't need to know, and you don't have a right to know."

He looked out the window and gave me a moment to calm down. "OK, leave it at that. Are you working?"

At least he changed the subject matter. "No Kelly, I have not worked now for maybe five years, I don't need to."

Kelly was shaking his head and looking at the floor. "Gees, if only I could say that, how much do you live on in a year?"

Again I was getting irritated. "Enough to live comfortably, and my wife can live just as comfortably."

Kelly then popped up sitting straight up in his chair. "Does your wife fool around?"

I started to get up. "What kind of a question is that?"

Kelly stood, reaching out and putting his hand on my shoulder. "Forget it, I was just curious."

I sat back down and then pointed my finger at him. "Kelly, you had better get to the point soon or I'm out of here. What the hell is up? Speak to me!"

He sat there shaking his head and then shrugged his shoulders and started to talk. "OK, Stan I have a game set up and if everything works right, it will mean more money than you and I have ever seen. If we play it right it can't fail and that is where you come in. Let me ask you this question. Where does your dad keep his money? I mean if he had a stash of money, where would he keep it?"

He got to the point alright and all I could do was sit there for a few seconds trying to grasp what he had just asked me. "What kind of question is that Kelly? Yeah, dad has money and he stashes a good part of it to avoid taxes."

He then turned toward the window. "OK, why don't you report that to the IRS?"

281

I was getting heated again. "Because Kelly, he is still my dad.

Kelly continued his conversation. "Even though he basically doesn't even recognize you as his child, he doesn't recognize your brothers and sisters either."

He had me there, but right now it makes little difference. "Yes."

Kelly was making his point and pressing me. "Come on Stan, are you telling me that you expect to inherit a share of his money?"

I stood my ground. "Yes."

Kelly was anticipating my answers and he knew he was pushing into some rather touchy areas. "Well you're consistent anyway. Stan, I can assure you that you will receive nothing from your father's estate. And, furthermore I can prove it."

He had thrown his most damaging punch and it got me square in the guts. I was stunned. "What the hell are you talking about?"

I had to admit that Kelly was good at working a person over with his words and he had me against the ropes this time. "Stan, it happened by chance. I was doing some research on a scheme I was working on when

I found this out on his funding web site. I was just fooling around on that site and I ran into your dad. Further research told me that he was in fact moving his money onto a small island called Fanning Island. It's an Atoll to the southwest of the Hawaiian Islands.

"Over the past three years he has moved no less than eighty percent of his listed holdings onto that Island. The notable thing about this place is that it has no treaties with the United States, nothing of any kind. Anything that goes there is protected from the poking around by the United States. It's a protected location and he is moving everything there."

This was news to me and it was big news. It was so big that he had my total undivided attention. Not only was this impossible, but if it was true I was screwed. "Why would he be doing that? What the hell is in Fanning Island that is worth anything?"

Kelly knew he had me now and it was just a matter of covering all the information and then progressing to his game. "I have no idea, all I know is that he is doing it and he is almost done. Stan I don't know what he is up to, but it's got to be big."

It took me several minutes to regain my composure. "Kelly I have one thing to ask you."

By this time he was smiling. He knew he had me, that I was interested, actually I was more than just interested, "Yeah."

I needed more information and I needed it now. "What the hell do you do for a living?"

Kelly let it all hang out and held nothing back. "Stan, I steal from people who have lots and would probably not miss a penny of it except for their greed. OK, I'm a crook. And, I learned a long time ago, never to pass up a chance at a sure thing. This is one of those things I cannot pass up. Then I thought of you and I figured you may want to know, so how about it?"

That was a stupid question, "So, how about what?"

He came back at me. "Are you in with me?"

My patience was almost worn through by this time, "In on what?"

Kelly was giving it to me a bit at a time. "Do you want to know what your father is doing with all his money?"

"And, if I did what good would it do me?"

He then dropped the bomb and sat back to see what would happen. "Well Stan, how about one hundred and fifty million dollars in your pocket?

I didn't believe him and told him so. "You have got to be joking? There is no way he is worth three hundred million, no way."

Kelly came back. "Well your dad has not told you or the rest of the family everything. To date he has transferred three hundred million in holdings and cash, to the island and it is sitting there waiting for him. The fact is, he has much more than that. How old is your dad?"

More questions, but now I was willing to answer. "I don't know maybe, sixty-five?"

He kept them coming. "Is he in good health?"

What else could I say except. "Yeah, I think so."

He then asked. "Is your mother alive?"

"No, we lost her two years ago."

He was driving in for the kill and I had no way to avoid it. "Then there is nothing to hold him here?"

I shot back. "Yeah, us kids."

He was up to the challenge. "Has he ever thought about you and your brothers and sisters before?"

What else could I say except. "No he hasn't, not really."

This guy was relentless and he drove his point home. "Well, then why would he suddenly start thinking about you now? Why would he want to get out of the U.S. at this time? Why would he pick a place like Fanning Island? What is there at Fanning that is advantageous for him to move everything there?"

"I don't, I don't have an answer for any of those questions, do you?" I was just about worn out and ready to quit and walk out.

He was ready to finish and finish he did. "Yeah Stan, I do. Fanning Island is the location of a money transfer point. It's a place where people with everything, want that little edge so that they can keep it all and then some. Your father is in the process of converting everything he has so that he can move out of the country and into a new life someplace else in this great big world of ours. The question is where is he going? And, last but not least, when is he going?"

He had me but I still had one question that needed answering. "And, where do I come into this big picture of yours?"

Kelly sat back and laid it out for me. "You are one of the few that can walk up to your father and ask him questions? You have access to him?"

Good question and he was right. "OK, I have access to him, but if he is actually doing this, he would never tell me, ever."

Kelly made his point and it was a good one. "I know that Stan, but you can get to him and that is the edge we need. Are you in on it?"

At that point I could see that Kelly was serious, more than serious, he was on a mission and he was not going to quit.

The invite was there for me, but I was still not sure. "Kelly, let me ask you one more question?"

"What's that?

"Is anyone going to get hurt? I mean is anyone going to get killed or seriously hurt?"

He became quiet for a few seconds and then looked right at me. "Stan, I can never guarantee that no one will get hurt, but I can say this. Your father will not be the one physically hurt. If anyone gets hurt it will be either you or I or both of us. Does that answer your question?"

"OK, I'm in." That was it; I took the step that he knew I would all along.

Can you believe it, I said I was in. My own father was the target, well his money anyway. I guess my reasoning was that Kelly was right. I was not destined to see any of dear old dad's money.

He was greedy beyond the meaning of the word. I was sure that he would figure a way to take it with him when he dies. Anyway, we had started the process and I was in it up to my neck. Little did I know just how far my neck was going to be pushed into this game?

Dear loving dad was not that happy to see me that day. He appeared to be preoccupied with something he was not willing to talk about. In fact, he could hardly wait for me to leave and showed it.

He jumped right at me. "Stan what are you here for, surely not to visit?"

I decided to be honest. "No dad, I need some help."

He sat there looking at me. "What's that?"

I started my story and knew I had to be careful. I was talking to the story king of investments and he could smell a fake clear across the room. "Well I am considering an investment and I'm not too sure just how to go about it."

"Fill me in." He was almost nonchalant in his response.

I began my story. "Well I have an opportunity to invest a set amount of money and see a real return on that investment in less than six months."

Whenever you talk money with dad it always got him excited and wanting to know everything about whatever it was so he could worm his way into it, if it was a real good game. "Alright, how much of an investment are you talking about?"

Kelly and I had worked a number up earlier. It had to be a number that made sense and was a big enough risk to convince him that I was into something real. To me it was a good number. "It would be around five million."

He sat there and quietly continued to ask me questions. That money brain was working overtime and I knew we had him when he asked, "The return?"

I hit him with the return figure straight on. "Right now about two and a half million plus my original five million investment."

He stepped into the trap. I should have been a little more careful because in my zeal to see him jump I didn't read his reaction right. "Can you invest more than five?"

"Yes, but the return percentage is not as good."

He sat there for several minutes looking at me, "Where Stan?"

He had a way of asking that simple two word question and he also had a way of putting the right amount of threat into it. "That, dear father, I am not ready to tell you."

He picked up his drink and took a sip and then sat back. "Trying to protect your investment?"

"Yeah, just like you taught me." I was nodding my head as I responded.

"OK, what's the angle?"

That was it. That was the question; the tip that we knew had to come and would have him in the box.

I continued. "It appears to be rather straight forward. I wire the funds to a selected location. At the same time a receipt of the transaction is certified and returned to me. My funds are not released until that certified receipt comes through. At that point the funds are released and I wait the six months for the return of my money and the interest promised."

He sat there and thought for a few minutes and then told me that it sounded too simple. I told him that was what caused me to come to him for advice. If it sounds too good to be true then it probably is not true, but there are occasions when in fact they are true and when that happens you can make a killing.

His mind was in high gear when he asked. "Is there a name for the company?"

I sat there for a few minutes. "Yes."

He was now reaching and pushing for the information that he wanted and needed. "Are you willing to tell me the name?"

Now was the time to spring the trap. "Dad, I don't want you to horn in on this. You've got all the money in the world and I'm just trying to improve my situation."

He took another sip of his drink. "Stan, you don't trust me?" He had kind of a hurt expression on his face.

I laid it out as it was. "Dad, that is the truth, I don't."

He shrugged it off and continued. "OK, let's see what we can glean from the facts that you have given me.

"First of all it sounds great and it does provide the security receipt with it. I liked the fact that the final transfer of the funds cannot take place until after the receipt is received and confirmed. That tells me that the company is a registered and reputable company. Those are all good signs.

"The problem is that this kind of an investment is usually considered a high risk transaction. You have no idea what is happening until you receive your payback and then it could be the whole thing or a small part to nothing of the original investment."

I was agreeing with him as he talked. "Yeah, I considered that."

He then asked. "Are you ready to dump five million?"

With that I shook my head. "I'm not ready to dump a buck let alone five million, but it looks good and I would love to increase my holdings. I guess the next question is this, are you willing to back me?"

Dad looked at me with a little surprise on his face, "How much?"

I countered with. "What would you be willing to go to?"

He stood his ground, "How much?"

So, I let him have it, "The full five million."

He sat back in his seat and shook his head while looking at me. "That figures, you're trying to make a bunch of money on my money. Why should I agree with that kind of a deal?"

I now had his attention. "I found it. If you want to invest more than the five million I would have no problem with that, but I would need the five million to get my share of the game."

You could see the wheels turning. He was almost ready to take the bait and he was starting to drool as well.

"How much will they accept top line?"

That was the bait question, what I had been hoping for; I needed to get ready to set the hook. "Gees, I'm not sure. I would have to check."

"Then do it and do it now." He was on the stalk now and that meant that I had him, but I had to remember. A shark on the hook is still a live shark.

I reached for the phone and made the call to the prearranged phone that we had set up. Knowing full well that dad's phone system recorded all outgoing numbers, we had set up a front phone to help convince him of the legitimacy of this game. When the phone was answered I turned to dad, "How much?"

He turned from the window, "Three hundred million."

I almost dropped the phone. "You have got to be kidding? You're not serious?"

My partner on the other end remained patient while I sealed the deal.

Dad walked over to me as I sat there holding the phone. "Son, when you work the system you do it with everything you have and I'm doing that right now."

I was trying to control myself. He had offered up a large part of his fortune for this game and I had not expected that. "Dad, you cannot afford to give up or lose three hundred million dollars. That is just crazy." That should have been a clue that something was going on in the back ground and I missed it.

He raised his hand and gestured for me to shut up. I returned to the phone and asked if a three hundred million dollar American would be acceptable. We held the line for about a minute and a half. Finally he returned and answered that with a "Yes that amount would be honored."

We then laid out the return for a funding of that size. Dad agreed.

This was way too easy. What we did not know was that dad was hyping his own game and we were about to become the sacrificial lambs in it. Good old dad, ready to put anyone on the line as long as it wasn't him.

When I got back to Kelly he was almost out of control. He was sure we had just pulled off the big one. I stood there looking at him. He was almost out of his mind.

"Kelly, there is a problem."

He stopped short. "What did you do?"

"Kelly, I didn't do anything. But, dad is acting strange and I don't like it. He was too willing, too ready to go, he knows something."

Kelly stopped short, "Are you sure?"

I was nodding my head. "You better damn well bet that I'm sure. There is something wrong here but I can't figure it out. When you found that web site did it require you to do anything to enter the site?"

Kelly thought a minute. "Well, yes, it asked me to register."

"And, how did you register?"

"I used a false name and then my e-mail address."

I was pressing now. "How old is your e-mail address?"

He sat there. "I change it every month and this was the first time I used it."

I could feel it and I was sure of it. "Kelly, there is something wrong here and we need to find out what it is before dear old dad makes his next move. Dad is a shark and when he smells blood he goes in for the kill, nothing can or will stop him. He has no moral or ethical feelings toward anyone opposing him, no matter whom they were and that included me.

"You told me that you found out that he was transferring three hundred million in cash to this Fanning Island. Is that right?"

"Yeah, that's right."

"And, when I approached him and he wanted to get in on the act he proposed three hundred million cash?"

"Yeah, that's right."

"Is that a coincident or happenstance."

He was starting to show signs of thinking again. "Yeah, I see what you mean."

I was now sure that a trap had been sprung, but dad was not the victim and I had a bad feeling that I was and probably Kelly as well. "Kelly, I never thought that dad had that much money, let alone having it in cash. There is something real strange going on here and we have to find out what it is. When he lands on us, we will pay with everything we have, including our lives."

Kelly still had not tied it all together as yet. "Come on Stan, he would never go that far?"

I knew my father and I knew that if anyone was going to be sacrificed, it would not be him no matter who he had to send to the slaughter house. "Kelly, I can assure that if there is any significant amount of money involved my dad is capable of just about anything. I am convinced that he was playing along with me and even more convinced that he knew what we were up to. On top of that I think it's too late for us to back out or get out of this thing. He's got us right where he wants us."

Kelly then asked. "Do you think he was after you all the time?"

I was thinking ahead by this time and knew that I had little time to mess around with too much thinking. "No, Kelly, he was waiting for anyone to find the web site and it ultimately turned out to be you and that brought me into it. The only leverage we have is that by chance it turned out to be me who approached him. He was expecting a stranger, not one of his own."

Kelly was still in denial. "OK, then way didn't he simply say no and end the game."

I knew I was in this thing deep. What was pissing me off was that Kelly didn't. "Because he wants to teach me a lesson and a hard one at that, my dad is a con man's con. He has made his fortune being a legal con man. There are more bodies lying behind him than you could ever count."

Kelly's eyes got big as he asked, "Dead bodies?"

Crap, this guy was too damn dumb to be doing this on his own. "No, business bodies, people he beat at their own games. He's a shark and he likes blood."

Kelly finally asked the question. "Well then, where do we go from here?"

I laid it out to him and reinforced it with a warning that his life was on the line.

"First off, we have maybe three days before he takes the next step. In that time we have to find out everything we can about Fanning Island, dad's movement of monies, and dads current financial situation. Everything, got me? So get your resources together and let's get hunting."

That old predator had gone fishing and Kelly turned out to be the fish that couldn't resist the bait. It was happenstance that brought us together after all. If it had been anyone else it would have simply been a target for my dad and he would have scored again. But, when I showed up it was his chance to take me down and he was going to do everything he could to do it.

I had always been the greater threat to my dad than any of the other kids in the family. He usually saved his most harsh actions and words for me. Always trying to cut me down and keep me out of the main stream of things. It was clear then as it is now that good old dad was scared to death of me and he was going to break me this final time.

Know what? He just may do it too. I had two handicaps; #1 was my lack of funding and #2 was Kelly. God, how did I fall for this one?

Fanning Island is a small island just southwest of Hawaii. It is part of the Republic of Kiribati and is about eleven miles long by seven miles wide. Total land area is around eight thousand five hundred acres including the marsh lands within the island ring. Population of the island is around one thousand natives. During most of the year tourists outnumber the natives by two or three to one. Beyond the tourist trade the island is the home of a Copra Plantation and other island fruit production.

So, what is special about Fanning Island? It's the location. That was it, the location. It sits right on the trade routes between South American and the Orient and The United States and Australia. That was the key. The majority of the world commerce passed over this part of the Pacific Ocean and that gave Fanning Island a step up in the world transportation systems.

So! What advantage does that give my father in the issue of commerce and financing? Absolutely nothing, why was he moving his money to Fanning Island, or was he really? We know that the web site Kelly found indicated that, but was he actually, or was that a rouse. What has Kelly stumbled into?

I had that stinging feeling running up my back by this time. I would imagine it was much like the feeling a prey has, just before the predator hits it. I had this feeling that I was a sitting duck and boy it does not feel good. It was just then that a thought hit me that almost floored me.

You know, that sudden shot of insight, when everything becomes clear, an epiphany. This was not a happenstance thing. It was a well calculated and designed event that in fact had me targeted from the very start.

It hit me like a sledgehammer. Kelly and dad were in this together. It had to be, there was no other explanation for this sudden and strange situation. Kelly did not just happen to think of me. He was targeting me all along. And, to make matters worse, my own dad was in on it, but, for only five million of my money. No, there was something more and I was going to find out what it was.

These conspiracy things usually drive me nuts. Most are based on stupid and unrelated events that the theorist pulls together and then stretches to the point where he thinks it makes sense. But, from time to time enough evidence comes along to clearly support and identify the conspiracy. In this case I feel it was the latter. That is the only logical conclusion that I can come to, based on what I now know. My most immediate need was to find out why.

Why are the two of them after me? Even more important, why were the two of them in partnership in this? What did they want to gain? How did I fit in to this thing? Knowing dad, this was not worth his efforts; there was something bigger here, much bigger.

OK, that's the issue and until something better comes up, that is the way I'm going to play it. It was vital that Kelly not figure out what I knew. So, I was going to play along with his greed and see where this thing was headed. I needed more information, much more.

I have never wanted or even considered killing someone before, but today I was ready to make an exception of Kelly. But, I wanted even more to nail him and especially with my dad in this game they were playing and in order to do that I would have to become a killer whale in an ocean of sharks.

Two hours later Kelly walked in. "Well, did you come up with anything useful?"

He walked over to the table and sat down and tossed a packet of paper onto the table in front of me. "I think we're in deep dodo."

I picked the packet up and started looking through it. It was perfect. Exactly what I expected it to be. Right down the line. That proved my suspicions were right, Kelly was a mole for my dad.

The papers indicated that dad was actually investing his money in an Australian firm via the Fanning Island bank. The Australian company was involved in an oil research project for the government in the North West of the country. The exact location was in the Northern Territory at a place called Perry's on the Daly which appeared to be located at the head waters of the Daly River and about fifty miles from the coast of the Bonaparte Basin in the southern area of the Timor Sea.

A quick run to the map showed that Perry's on the Daly was located in the mountains of that territory. In Australia anything over a hundred feet is a mountain and these are no different. They are more like foothills to us and when you consider the rest of the terrain in that area, it could well be oil country. I had never heard of it. A chill went up my back.

The papers had all my questions answered, just that they were too detailed and too perfect. Kelly had made a mistake and I would use it to my advantage.

One thing I knew about the Australian Government was that it did not like sharing its resources with outside money. It had no problem with its native companies working outside the country and in the resources of other countries, but it did have a problem when that money was directly related to its own resources. That would be my ace in the hole. Maybe, just maybe, good old dad had just dug himself into a corner. Now it was my turn to use Kelly. Poor dumb SOB.

Australia had always held a warm spot in my heart. I had been there several times and had made a number of friends from Perth to Sidney. You know, guys and gals I spent time with on the beach, and partying. Some had a substantial amount of money and others just got along. The point is I had a well-rounded acquaintance with a lot of people in the know and with influence.

I told Kelly that I needed a few hours to think this over. I was not sure as to what I was getting into and felt that I needed some quiet time in order to work it out. The look in Kelly's eyes told me that I had pushed the right button. He bought it and left.

I knew that someone would be watching me. Dad would never trust Kelly in everything. Knowing dad, he had someone on Kelly. Whoever that was would clearly have complete and total control over everything that Kelly did and what his final actions were. He would do the same with me if everything worked out as he had planned.

I now needed to find a place to work up my next move without being obvious and still have the privacy I needed to do what had to be done. My own home was of no use because I knew they had it bugged. They had to. They had to keep tabs on my every move. This was the critical part of the plan and my movements would tell the whole story.

I went to a store I had heard of and purchased an RF Detector and then went back to my place and started a scan of the entire residence. Sure as hell I found them. They had every room in the house bugged including my phones.

So, I went to the library. If there is one place where you can find all the resources you need for this type of a situation it is the place. For someone doing research that is what it is all about. I used the library a lot in my business days, so I was no stranger to it and dad knew I would go there to pursue this thing. So, I did.

Theodore R. Langdon, Teddy for short, was probably the most dependable and influential Australian I knew. He had his finger into just about anything that involved money and Australia. That was going to be the key to my plan; Teddy was my resource and my connection to the government down under.

I finally had all I needed and I called Australia, specifically Teddy. When I asked Teddy about the oil situation in the Northern Territory, he went completely quiet on me. "Teddy, what's up?"

There was an unusually long pause before he came back to me. "Stan, no one is supposed to know about that."

I felt that chill again. "Teddy, I need to talk to you about this. Something is going on here that tells me there is something really big coming out of that territory. Can you give me anything on it?" As I talked to him I became even more convinced that this thing was big and that I was in real danger. "Teddy, I kid you not, this means my life if I get too far into this thing. I have a really bad feeling about it."

Teddy remained quiet for another minute and then told me, "You should my friend that you should. You have just stumbled onto one of the greatest secretes and issues of this country. Just knowing the location as you stated could get you killed down here."

At this point I knew that I could trust no one, but I had to trust someone. There was no way around it. "Teddy, I am not involved in that location, but I have been drawn into a situation, and I am sure that I am being set up as the sacrificial lamb in this case.

"There is some big money on the way down there, like three hundred million in American. Did you know of that?"

There again was a pause and this time Teddy cleared his throat. "No way, that can't be Stan. That project is closed off to any outside money. Are you sure?"

Now there were two of us under the gun and both in the same boat. That being the case, neither one of us had that much information about what was going on. "Yeah, I'm about as sure as I can be. Let me fill you in on what has happened."

Twenty minutes later Teddy was exhaling. "Stan, you are sitting with your head on the block and the knife is already on its way down."

That I already knew. "Yeah, I get that impression. They are trying to get me to slide five million in on the deal and if and when I do that it will become known to your government, quite by accident of course. With that my head will roll as a perfect cover for the bulk of the money that is being targeted on that project. To make matters worse Teddy, its being orchestrated by my father."

"Damn, that's too bad Stan. What do you want me to do?"

I then laid it on the line. "Well first of all, you need to know that this is probably going to get violent over here once good old dad learns of what I've done to him. It could come back on you through the company over there. Do you know that?"

Ted paused, "I know."

I continued to fill him in but first I gave him the chance to back out right now. "Teddy, if this is too much for you, say so. I'll hold nothing against you on this. I do not expect you to sacrifice anything in this situation."

When he came back to me, he was something more than good old Teddy. He was determined. "Hold on Stan, this is directly involving me, my company, my government, and our resources. I take exception to anyone trying to manipulate it for their own gain. I'm with you. What do you want?"

For the next hour Teddy and I laid out our next moves. After I hung up he would start the process there. We had a seventeen hour time difference to work with so I knew I had to stay on top of things in order for this to work out.

Teddy had considerable interest in the oil industry in Australia, but none in this particular company. Rumor had it that this company had a direct tie to China, but so far there had been no clear documentation on that. This situation may bust that issue wide open.

I left Teddy with his part of the plan to carry out and set out to complete mine. That is making me an even bigger target for good old dad. I was going to walk right into his trap, and play it there all the way. My life was now in Teddy's hands and I sure as hell hoped I had made the right decision.

Kelly arrived as I knew he would and I agreed with his take on the situation and we set out to pull a fast one on dad. In actuality, Kelly was getting ready to pull his knife out and give it to me in the back.

I had to admire dad for his resourcefulness in this whole thing. He found a great investment, though it would be illegal as all get out. He found the perfect scapegoat in Kelly. If everything hit the deck, Kelly was the perfect one to nail. His past history would work perfectly into this situation, and dad could walk away free and easy and probably save every penny he was trying to invest in this thing.

He was spending a considerable amount of money upfront with the bugging of my place and probably Kelly's as well. The tracking teams he had assigned to Kelly and me were good, but not the best. I had the green Ford four door spotted within three blocks. What really concerned me were the two guys in the green Ford. They were good sized guys and could make quick work of me.

I still could not help the feeling that I had missed something. You know that gnawing feeling that eats away at your insides. There was something I needed to deal with before we got too much further into this game. What had I missed? What did I fail to do? Where was my weakest link? Teddy!

Damn, I knew better. Teddy had said he had considerable oil interests, but none in this company. That should have alerted me. It was oil and whether one had direct involvement in any company made little or no difference, the connection, the link was OIL. I had placed all my eggs in Teddy, and now I knew they were about to make an omelet out of me, a meat one for that matter.

I got up and walked across the room to Kelly and grabbed him by the front of his jacket and jerked him out of his chair. "You dirty stinking pig. How could you get me into something like this?"

Kelly's face went white as a sheet. He started to stammer and tried to pull my hands off of his jacket, but I was beyond mad as hell and short of killing temper.

"I had to," he said. "If I had refused he was going to have my liver cut out."

If I had gotten any closer to him I would have been inside his clothes, "Who, damn you, who?"

He was coming apart at the seams, "Your dad, who else."

I kept pushing him with everything I had. "Why, Kelly? You better start talking and talking fast. You have just minutes to live and what you say just may save your life."

His eyes were huge and the tears were pouring out of them. "God, man, he caught me trying to pull a scam on one of his close friends. He sent two guys over to my place and they had a heart to heart talk with me.

I took the living side of their suggestions. Your dad needed a sacrifice, a scapegoat for this scam he was working on and he had picked you. I just happened to come along at the right time and he decided to use me to get to you.

"Honestly Stan, I was fighting for my life. There was no way I could say no."

I had him now and I pushed for all of it. "How much is he paying you?"

He got the phony look of surprise on his face, "Pay? Come on Stan I wouldn't take money for something like this?"

I poured it to him with everything I had. "Kelly, you would take money for your little sister, now, how much?"

He took a huge gulp. "Two hundred and fifty thousand, that's all."

That made me even madder than I had been. "You stinking scum bag. You sold me out and it could well get me killed. You have no idea what this does to you do you?"

"What do you mean?"

"You think he is going to give you money like that? Hell no he isn't. You are about to be the guy that killed his beloved son, you idiot."

By now he was scared and confused and could only say. "What?"

I had it all figured by this time and so I cut loose and let him have it all. "Yeah, he has planned this thing all the way. No one would ever believe that he would kill his son over a commercial venture. But a con caught in the act may well do it.

"He didn't need my five million. That was never even considered. He wanted my body and your hands with my blood all over them to insure his money would clear any problems that may develop in the Australian thing. He needed to be able to say he had been scammed and scammed by you and when he found out, after giving over the three hundred million, you killed his son to try and keep him from going public and getting his money back.

"It was the perfect layout. If his investment cleared all the hurdles he stood to double or triple it. If something went wrong and the government caught on then he could claim he had been scammed and the scammer had killed his son. He never meant it to go this way. He thought the investment was above board and he had invested in good faith.

"To make it even more believable his doctor would testify that he was mentally weaker than he had been two to five years ago. That he was developing dementia and that he had ventured out on this thing believing he was doing the right thing. In other words he had been victimized two times. His son had been killed and the killer had tried to scam him out of his life's work.

"Oh, and dad, you can go to hell."

When I said that, Kelly turned around expecting to see the old man standing at the door. "What?"

314

I started to laugh. "He has the place bugged Kelly. Now, get your ass out of here and in your car and run for your life. You'll be lucky to make it to the city limits. Oh, and Kelly, don't ever show your face around here again. Now, get the hell out."

Kelly stood there a few seconds and then a look of amazed understanding came across his face and he turned and headed out the door.

I started to turn around in the room. "Dad, I know you're listening. Call Teddy and advise him it did not work out. I'm out of this thing and you can go to hell. I'm going to leave now and you can have your people go to my place and pull the bugs, all of them. I'll be checking the house when I get back. I'll be out of town for a week or so. Keep in touch you old fart."

I left the resort and went on home and packed a few things, got my passport and headed for Australia. I had a few words for Teddy, and they were going to be interesting. No one tried to stop me from leaving my apartment or the country. I'm sure dad let Teddy know that I was coming, so I expected to be met at the arrival gate. We would see.

My arrival at Sidney was uneventful. I took a taxi to the Hotel and settled in. If I had it figured right I would be having company in about thirty minutes.

Sure enough there was the expected knock on the door. When I opened the door I was shocked to find Teddy and his girlfriend Ruth standing there. "Teddy, I expected someone else to appear here, not you, and Ruth, I'm glad to see you."

They pushed their way into the room and we retreated to the sitting area and sat down. I sat there and waited. One of them had to speak before too long, I know I had nothing to say at the time.

Teddy finally broke the silence. "Stan, this whole thing was unnecessary. There was no reason for you to come down here, none whatsoever."

I took my time and played my cards carefully. "Teddy tell me this, you don't think five million is nothing do you Teddy?"

He countered. "You lost nothing Stan."

I snapped my head up. "Teddy I almost lost everything and you were tied up in it up to you neck.

"Damn it to hell man, I thought you were my friend. But, my biggest error was

316

calling you in the first place. When you said oil I knew that I had called the wrong person. Oil is as oil does and you're one and the same with it. You sold your nation out Teddy. You took my dad's offer and sold everyone out. How much did he give you, how much Teddy?"

He sat there looking at me and calculating just how much he should say to me. "He gave me ten percent of the profits."

I looked at him in amazement. "And, that would come to an estimated?"

He then leaned back. "That's around a billion and a half a year for the rest of my life, Stan."

I had not expected that and I was clearly impressed. "Well Teddy, I came here to queer the whole thing."

He looked over at Ruth. "Stan, it's too late. The purpose of this whole game was to draw the attention of our competition away from Perry's on the Daly for just one month. When the word got out of the struggle taking place on Fanning Island, everyone's attention was drawn to that location. It was a classic father and son match.

"Meanwhile, the main event was progressing as planned. Perry's on the Daly is on its way and cannot be stopped. A massive amount of money has gone into this show and it is now beyond any government intervention or international intervention. A lot of money had been made over the last thirty days. Your dad is now one of the wealthiest men in the world. Needless to say, I am so well off that there is nothing I cannot have.

"And, you my dear Stan will find a rather large sum of money sitting in your account back in Harper Beach. Oh, and your wife has discovered a hefty little sum in her accounts as well. It's over Stan, let it ride."

I sat there. There was little I felt, or I wanted to say at that point, but something had to be said. "Teddy, right now I want to punch you square in the face. I want so badly to leave you lying in a pool of blood. You don't know how good it would feel to nail you right now."

There was a long pause and then Ruth opened her mouth and what came out put me square in my chair. "OK Teddy, that's enough. Listen to me Stan, and hear what I am saying. It is over, got it. Over! You can run around crying about anything and everything and it will change nothing.

"The acquisition of the Perry's on the Daly land has been done and is complete. I own one hundred percent of it. My company will start drilling next month and we will open that entire region up to oil exploration.

"Your father and I have been close on this situation for years and thanks to his best efforts he came up with a plan that would draw everyone away from the Northern Territory for the amount of time I needed to close the deals. They are closed. It is mine. Nothing can change that. Get it?"

Teddy shrugged his shoulders and nodded. "It's all done Stan. She holds all the cards and no one can change that."

I couldn't believe it and then I thought of Kelly. "What about Kelly?"

She looked straight at me. "He's expendable."

Talk about a black widow, poor Kelly. He was suckered in by my dad and in turn suckered me in and we became front stage center in this whole gimmick. What a move.

Kelly always seemed to get busted up one way or the other. No matter what he got into he would always come out with something broken. He was just that way. They found him in his car about five miles out of town. He had been speeding and lost control and hit the only tree for ten miles in any direction. They said he died instantly. Yeah, right, he was probably already dead when his car hit the tree…

"You see Delbert life goes on no matter what comes and goes from Duker's Store. In this case Stan came here to the Store to try and find some means of protecting himself. How he ended up here was his issue not ours, but once here then the information he needed was given to him. In his case the issue was that one small piece of physical hardware.

"In Stan's situation it was not the future or the past that was the issue but it was location. His need for an answer is what brought him all the way here to this store. In the end his needs were met and he became that much wealthier.

I sat there thinking over this last story. As strange as it was I knew what Frank was trying to communicate to me. Duker's Store had fulfilled a need for Stan and even though someone eventually died the item provided saved the life of the one who had been seeking it.

I was really beginning to understand what was going on here. Duker's Store was much more than a simple little country store where dreams were pursued and lives were changed. It was the past, present, and future for anyone of the seven billion people living on this planet. All any of them need do was come to the store and seek that which they needed to build their life with.

Chapter Eleven

Carl Dixon

I had finally reached the point where I knew why I was there at Duker's Store and that I would remain there for however long I was needed. It had taken Frank some time to finally get me to accept my situation and now that I had I was ready to move on.

It was then he turned to me. "Delbert, there is one more situation I feel you need to hear before we take the next and final step in my retirement. This situation is tied to that item sitting on the top shelf over there by the door.

If you take a close look at it, you will see it is one of those laser pointers lights people love to play with all the time. However, there is a difference and that is this pointer was used as a weapon and not a toy or a tool.

When you hear this story you will see that Duker's Store is much more than a simple have-it-all store. No this store is a place where worlds can be change or saved, where people can find the resources to achieve what they needed. In this case Carl needed twenty-five thousand laser lights and Duker's Store was the only place he could get them in any reasonable time frame.

…It's terrifying! I can think of nothing more terrifying than the black of night. As a child I was deeply troubled by the dark of night. I could not sleep in a dark room, or walk a dark street. My imagination would simply run away with me and in short order I would be trembling and near tears.

What was it that caused me to have such a fear of the dark? It was no different from the day except the light was gone. Everything else was the same. The same bed, same closet door, same windows, same lights, and so on. The only difference was the light was gone and darkness was there.

I would lay there in my bed and look into the darkness and think I could see things, something moving around in that darkness. I knew nothing could be there, but yet I was sure I could see them.

When looking into the darkness it is not all the same level or intensity of darkness. Believe it or not there are shadows in darkness. Any solid mass had a deeper degree or level of darkness. The open air around it would be of a lesser degree or level of darkness.

I studied darkness night after night trying to determine if something was actually there. I would turn my flashlight on directed toward the middle of the room and nothing was there. Yet, the darkness around the light appeared to still have something moving within it. All my childhood years, I faced that issue and never came up with an answer other than my belief there was something there, something alive.

Even today I have that back of the neck feeling something is there, something I don't want to meet, but something that is trying to meet me. As a thirty-five-year-old man I could still feel the fear that gripped me in those years of my childhood. I still hated to go out into the darkness and hated walking into a dark room.

That's why on the evening of the First of September in 1996 I found myself standing at the doorway of an office in the building where I worked. The office was in the interior with no outside windows. Something had just grabbed the back of my hand and I knew things were not right.

The light switch was just inside the door to my left and as I reached into the room to turn the lights on, something grabbed my hand and pushed it away. The shock of feeling something grab me from out of the black of that room almost put me down.

Yet, at the same time I realized the manner in which it grabbed me was not violent or aggressive. It was more like someone taking a hold of my hand and tenderly moving it back toward the door.

I hadn't even been looking into the room, know what I mean. I had some papers in my left hand and was busy looking them over, and when I got to the room I reached in like I had done a thousand times to turn the light on.

We never closed the door unless we had a meeting of some kind going on otherwise it stood open all the time. I saw nothing but I felt it touch me and push or maybe set my hand away from the light switch.

Yes it scared the hell out of me, and I just didn't know what was going on. I felt it touch my hand and then a cold flush went charging through my body. It left me shaken and somewhat out of breath.

I stood there in total amazement for maybe thirty to forty-five seconds and then decided to try again. I slowly reached into the room for the switch and again something took hold of my hand and pushed it back. I stepped back to the middle of the hallway. "Allen is that you?" No answer. I then asked; "Becky, is that you?" No response.

As I stood there looking into the darkness I could see it, a mass with no recognizable shape to it, yet it was there. It was about my size in height and width. Other than that there were no discernible features to it. I remembered I had a small light in my pocket on my key chain. You know, one of those light fobs that are used to see the key hole in your car when you are trying to unlock it. I pulled it out and turned it on.

As the light hit the inside of the room there was a movement that appeared as if something was diving or dodging away from the light. It was so fast I thought for a second I had not actually seen it, but no, it was there. There was no doubt about it, there was something in that room and it was something that avoided light.

That's stupid! That cannot be. There is no way anything is in that room other than an employee trying to play with me or some rodent that has gotten into the offices. Yet, my mind told me it was there. So, what was I going to do? Stand here in the hallway the rest of the night or go in and get the papers I came here for?

Yet, I knew I was not going into that room at this time. My mind went back to those nights in my room as I contemplated all the different kinds and types of creatures that roamed and lived in the darkness, a whole different universe from the one of light. A place that only existed once the light was extinguished. A place that only brave men ventured into and I did not feel brave right this moment.

This is dumb. There is nothing in that room that can hurt me or bother me. Nothing!

Yet, there it was, standing just inside the door and away from the lights of the hallway just outside the room. Not only could I see it, but I knew it was looking at me, sizing me up, determining what and who I was.

As I stood there looking into the room I did not hear or see Dave as he walked up to me. My eyes and mind were riveted to the creature inside the room.

"What's up Carl?"

I almost messed myself. I think I had run ten or fifteen feet down the hall before I realized it was Dave and not the creature from inside the room.

Dave looked at me. "Carl, are you all right?"

As he did that he reached into the office and turned on the light. "Man you look white as a sheet. Are you feeling alright?"

I finally collected myself and responded to him. All the while moving back to the door and looking into the office. "Yeah, I'm alright. You just scared the crap out of me. I was thinking about something else and did not see you come in. Boy, did you give me a shock."

We walked into the office as I took a long hard look around the place. Everything was as it should have been. I walked over to my desk and got my papers and turned to head out. Dave looked at me again and again asked if I was alright.

"Dave I was in a total state of concentration and didn't see you coming down the hall. When you spoke up it caught me by surprise and scared the hell out of me. That's all there was to it."

Besides there was no way in hell I was going to tell him what I had just seen. Especially after he had walked into the room and turned on the light. After a few minutes of small talk I excused myself and left the office and building.

Damn, that was embarrassing as hell. I wasn't going to tell him about seeing something that wasn't there. What else could I do? I came down here to get those papers and I had them in hand and so I left making sure to avoid any dark areas on my way to the parking lot. I even turned the interior lights on before I got in the car.

With that I headed home and by the time I got there twenty minutes later I had pushed the whole incident to the back of my mind. That was Sunday night about nine thirty.

That following Monday morning I showed up for work as usual. I knew something was going on when I turned in to the parking lot. The place was crawling with police. I parked my car and walked toward the front door of the building where a group of people were standing. Strange, they were all from my office, every one of them.

I walked up to the group and saw Steve standing there and went over to him. "What's going on here?"

Steve turned and recognized me, "Hi Carl."

I again asked. "Steve what's up?"

Steve moved closer to me and lowered his voice while leaning toward my right ear. "They found Dave in the office this morning dead."

The word dead hit me like being hit with a baseball bat. It literally staggered me to the point Steve had to reach out and steady me. "What!"

Steve was looking me in the face and replied. "Yeah, they found Dave dead up in the office."

I must have looked terrible at that point. I know I felt terrible. I was finally able to say. "That can't be, I saw Dave in the office last night as I was picking up some papers for a presentation I had to have done this week."

Steve took my arm and turned me toward him. "You saw Dave?"

I continued what I was saying. "Yeah, I was standing at the door of the office when he walked up to me. Darn near scared me to death. We both went in and I got my papers and left. He was sitting at his desk as I walked out the door."

"Carl, you need to talk to the police about this."

"OK, I'll head right up there now."

The officer at the door stopped me until I explained to him, I had seen the victim that last evening, in our joint office. The officer made a call and then told me to go on upstairs to our main office reception area where a detective would meet me.

As I came through the door into the reception area Detective James walked up to me and introduced himself. "Mr. Dixon, it is Mr. Dixon isn't it?"

I took his hand. "Yes."

The detective released my hand. "As I understand it you say you saw Mr. Fulman last night in your joint office."

I was nodding my head. "Yeah, I was there to get some paper work for the next week and he was there to work up a report due this morning."

"Did you see anything else that was out of the ordinary? Something that is not normal for this building or location?"

I sat there a few seconds. "No sir. We talked and then I left. He was still in the office the last I saw him."

The next question was a little bothersome but I knew the officer had to pursue each and every issue he came across. "Were you and Mr. Fulman on good terms, by that I mean did you get along?"

Even though I knew he needed to ask these questions it still bothered me. "Yeah, we did. We have worked together in that office for the last ten years. His kids are close to my kids and our wives spend a lot of time together. What happened here anyway?"

The detective looked at me and then sat back and took a deep breath. "Well, Mr. Dixon, it appears your friend ran into a rather unpleasant individual or group of individuals. Every bone in his body has been broken. He has been completely crushed from head to toe. Even more interesting is that there is absolutely no signed of a struggle or fight of any kind. It's almost as if someone or something had wrapped itself around him and crushed him. Even more important, there is not a drop of blood, or any fluids on or near the body. He must have died in seconds."

By this time I was getting dizzy and had to lie back before I fell down.

"Mr. Dixon, do you need a drink?"

I waved my right hand at him. "No, it's just that I can't believe this could happen to Dave. God, what's his family going to do?"

"I can't answer that for you sir, but I do know we don't know what we're going to tell her at this point. So far the coroner has no idea as to what the cause of death is. All he knows is, the victim was crushed. How and by whom, we have no idea.

"Mr. Dixon, we need you to give us everything you can think of in regards to what happened last evening while you and Mr. Fulman were together. And by everything I mean in detail."

I related to the detective when I had arrived at the office and that I was standing in the hallway, just preparing to go into the office when Dave walked up. "We stood there and talked for a few minutes and then he walked into the office and I followed. There was no one else in the office and I saw no one else in the overall office area.

"He went to his desk and sat down and I went to mine and got the paper work and started to walk out. The last thing we said to each other was that we would see each other in the morning. That's it. There was nothing else. As I walked out of the building I saw Dave's car parked next to mine and no other cars in the lot. I got in my car and left."

Just between you and me I was not going to tell them of my encounter with the shadow figure prior to Dave's getting there. Just at that time another detective came bursting through the door and told Detective James, "We found another one."

Detective James turned, "Another what?"

The other officer looked at me and then back to Detective James, "Body, we found another body, upstairs in the office just over this one."

Detective James was almost speechless, "No way!" He jumped up and hit the door at a run.

Within five seconds I found myself sitting in the reception area all by myself. The place went crazy. There were people running all over the place. The order had been given to check each and every office, closet, storage room or utility room in the building. Everything was to be checked.

It was just about that time I had a sense of heaviness settle over me. I knew the image I had seen last night was involved in this thing and now two people were dead. Why had it not attacked me? Instead it had pushed my hand away from the light switch as a mother would a child reaching out to touch a candle. And now, two people were dead.

Several minutes later Detective James returned to me and told me I could leave. If they needed anything else, they would contact me.

As I walked out of the building I was assaulted by the media wanting to know what was going on inside the office building. I played dumb and moved through them and over to my fellow employees.

My boss, Mr. Fix, walked up and asked me what was happening inside. I asked if he knew about Dave and he said he did. "Well, they found another body upstairs in the office over the one Dave was killed in."

Mr. Fix went white and almost fell down. I grabbed him and helped him over to a bench and sat him down. "Sir, I think it best we not open the office today. Maybe we should send everyone home for the time being."

He agreed and I advised everyone to take the day off and we would be in touch later on.

I needed to go somewhere and think this thing out. Something was wrong and I had the strange feeling I was mixed up in it up to my neck.

What was that thing I had seen last evening? Did it have anything to do with Dave's death? Is there anything I can do to correct or shed some light on this mystery? There had to be an answer if for no other reason than to bring some semblance of reality back into my life. One thing I knew, I was going to have to face that thing head on. And, that was causing me to question the reality of this whole situation.

The question that came to my mind, was this the same creature I saw, found in any dark room I entered or is it located in only one place? That I did not know, so the reality of this situation was I was going to have to go back to the office and face it there. Maybe, just maybe I will find some answers.

That following Friday evening I headed for the office. I knew I had to overcome my fear of the dark to deal with this. I knew I may not come home from this thing once I get into the room. Yet, I had to. I had to find out if that thing was the thing responsible for what happened to my friend. I was not prepared for what was to come. If I had known ahead of time, I would have quit my job and moved out of the area all together.

As I walked down the hallway I felt the skin on the back of my neck start to creep. The door was standing open as usual. As I stepped around and in front of the door and looked into the darkness it came into view. We stood there on both sides of the threshold looking at one another. That is if it could look as we know it. As I watched it I could see others moving around in the darkness behind it. There was not just one, but how many others were there?

Well, here we are. It's over there and I'm standing here. All I had to do was step across the threshold. Obviously it was not going to even if it could. I reached out and pushed my hand into the darkness and immediately felt it take a hold of my hand. There was no pulling just a holding on, like it was trying to assist me into the darkness.

All the fear and terror of my childhood rushed in on me. The unknown and the blackness blasted through me. I wanted to turn and run, but it had a hold of my hand and with a gentleness and firmness it pulled me into the darkness, into the unknown.

We have all felt and done it. Done something new that we had never done or thought we would ever do before. Here I was standing inside that room away from the light and feeling the darkness envelop me. Yet, this was a different darkness than I was accustomed to. It was darkness with substance. It had mass, it had sensitivity. It was clearly alive and controlling. I waited for my vision to adjust to the lack of light and then when it started to adjust I started to see all that was present.

They were all over in the room. Besides the one I had been looking at and was holding onto my hand there were big ones and little ones everywhere. All of them were looking at me, well I had the feeling they were looking at me. It was true; there is life and living creatures in the darkness, lots of them.

We stood there for several minutes as I worked to overcome my fear and for my eyes to finish adjusting to the darkness. It was then I noted that many of those present were not looking my way, but were in fact looking out and away from us. As if they were on guard duty.

It was at this point I started to hear the whispering, the sounds of someone or something talking quietly to me. In a tone of voice that was alien to me, but still understandable and comforting. It was just a few seconds until I realized the voice was coming from the creature that was still holding my hand. I listened closely and finally understood. "Can you hear me?"

I felt my head tilt first to the left and then to the right. "Yes, I do."

The creature then asked me to sit down and listen carefully, they had much to tell me and I needed to remember just what is being related to me.

"What is going on here?"

The voice then came back. "We have much to tell you and you must be ready to act on what we tell you. If you do not then the world as we know it will end. The region of darkness was making its move and if it was successful all of mankind would end. A major problem had manifested there in the darkness and it had to be addressed before it grew any larger than it has."

I then asked the obvious; "Why are you doing this?"

Whatever this creature was it continued to explain the situation to me. "We are beings of the night of darkness. We cannot live in light in that it will destroy us. We are a civilization that has no desire to interfere in the life and wellbeing of those of the light side. The two were never meant to meet and be in a relationship. Yet, there are those among us who desire to feed on the light side. They have a deep hate for the light side and will do anything to destroy it.

"When we look into the light we see as you do the dark side. There is something there, but we cannot get a clear view of them. Do you remember, when you were a child being fearful of the dark and feeling there was something there just out of reach?"

Yes I remembered those nights, many of them. "Yes I do. I have had a great fear of the dark all my life."

"Well we are the same way with light. In the past multiple times we have developed a means of seeing into the light and seeing the beings that live there. We have been watching you for a number of years. It was by that means the Devourers started to take advantage of our discovery."

"Devourers?"

"Yes, that is what we are contacting you for. These are creatures of our realm that live on the life force of other beings. Normally, they are predatory toward the rest of us in this realm, but recently they have become more aggressive toward the light side inhabitants.

"In the last duplex they attacked and caught their first light side beings. They did this by getting the beings to come back into a dark area and then taking their life from them."

As I listened to the creature I started to think about Dave. "In other words, you're telling me that they crush the life out of them and leave them with every bone in their body broken?"

"Yes, that is true. The Devourers cannot live in the light just as we cannot. So they had to develop a way of drawing the light beings into the dark."

I didn't like what I was hearing but needed to hear more. "And, how was that done? Can you be more specific for me, how do they do it?"

"We are sure, at this time, they are using a black flash. All we know is they have developed it and they took light creatures the last duplex. With that, others will start falling all across the face of this world."

That matched what had happened to Dave and I needed to know much more. "OK, as I understand this situation, you have approached me to bring the dark side and the light side together so we can fight a common enemy, right?"

"That's right. You need to know what is happening and if you can build a defense against the Devourers then maybe, just maybe we can use it on the dark side ourselves. We would like nothing better than to eliminate the Devourers all together. Your survival will be ours as well."

"How do I know you're honorable and in reality, you're not the Devourers yourself?"

"If we were the Devourers you would never have got this far. We would have crushed your life out of you before you knew what was going on. Listen to me. You have wondered about the darkness for all your life. As a child you feared the darkness and as a grown being you still fear the darkness. You knew that something lived in this realm and it was always there and moving around you.

"We have watched you over these many multiples and have come to know you well. Right now, your fear level is extremely high and you know just by our touch we are not a threat to you. We have protected you all these multiples in the hopes that one day you would be able to help us. The same is true for many others across your world who live in the light side.

A good number of our fellow beings have lost their life force while protecting you so that one day you could help us remove the scourge from the face of our world. Do not fall away from us; we have too much invested in you.

"Please, you must help us and in doing that you will help yourself as well as your world. The Devourers are moving and will stop at nothing to achieve their goals and that goal is the domination of your world. They will feed on you as you feed on a field of your corn or, a herd of your cattle. Once they get to that point there is no hope for us. They will increase in number and will eventually eliminate us before we can them.

"Now you must know here and now. Watch for the black flash. That is how they draw you in, they set off a black flash and when it goes off that usually results in the light being going into the dark room close by and they pounce."

"A black flash?"

"Yes, you will see it much as you see a light flash when a light beam passes across a window."

"OK, you mean like a flash from a camera?"

"Yes, that is right."

"They will try to get you once they learn we have made contact. They will use the black flash to try and get you to come to them. Stay away and live. Now, here is what we need and hope you can bring to us this next duplex."

"You mean the next day?"

"Yes, that's it, the next day."

"OK let's have it. Wait, answer me this question. How are you communicating with me? How do you know our language?"

"We are not talking to you in a loud voice as you do between one another. You are hearing us in your mind. We have learned your language over the many multiples we have lived next to each other. We can do that because you vocalize your language. We do not. We communicate mind to mind. We needed to achieve that level with you and found you were the most likely individual from the light side that could receive our communications."

"So, if I brought someone with me to talk to you, they would not be able to? Nor would they be able to see you?"

"That is somewhat correct. Those of you who have feared the dark and believed beings were there would be able to hear and see us. You have learned over the many multiples what to look for and what you are seeing. The rest just fell into place."

"OK, what's our plan?"

"The only thing that can destroy a Devourer is light, the same light that will destroy each of us here on the black side. So we need some form of light projection that can be precisely aimed or directed at a particular spot. This light source must also be limited, that is its range cannot be too extensive. If it is too far, then the light can pass through your wall and into other areas of the black side and kill the innocent."

I stood there listening to it. "Let me get this right. I need to come up with a light weapon you can aim, that is precise and does not have an extended range. That may be one hell of a request. But, I think I have an idea as to what it is we really need. The next question is how do we get the Devourers to come to me? Remember, I am just one individual and there are probably many Devourers."

"Carl you don't understand. We want the weapons so we can use them against the Devourers. With a weapon that shoots a controlled beam of light we can hold it and not have the light touch us. In that way we can attack and finally eliminate them once and for all. Do you understand? You are not meant to be in the fight. That is our responsibility. We will carry the battle to the Devourers and bring their reign of terror to an end."

That was comforting except for one thing. "Hold on just a minute. I know you will not like what I am about to say, but please hear me out. For me to just turn some weapons over to you causes' me a considerable amount of concern. I still am not totally convinced about what you have said.

"But, I need to warn you that any light weapon I bring to you will not be effective on those of us on the light side. Do you understand that? If this whole thing is a con to get me to supply weapons that can be used to attack my own world, it will not work."

It clearly was tracking with me. "We understand your concern and caution, but I can assure you, your fear is unfounded. There is nothing the light side can do for us. Destroying it would be of no benefit to the black side at all. Light would still exist from the area above us. We would gain nothing. We will accept any light weapon you can provide us with."

"Alright, say I agree and will supply you with the weapons. How many will you need? Second, how will you attack the Devourers? Third, how long will it take?"

It was being patient with me now. "Clearly Carl, you don't understand the black side and we recognize that. Darkness is everywhere and we beings can travel through it to any place it is present at will. A room can be filled with light and as soon as it goes off, those of us wanting to be there will be there. I can decide I want to be at any point in your world and when darkness comes over it, I am there. We live in an entirely different universe from you. We come in contact because light and dark meet all the time, each bumping into the other time and again throughout all of time and creation.

"With you, travel is more difficult, you must have machines and power to move across the face of the world. You are not made of light, but for us, we are part of darkness and we move freely through it."

All right that was interesting. "Then you have been in my bedroom over many years? I think maybe our year is one of your multiples."

"Yes, you are right. Yes, I have been in your bedroom for many years."

"Why?" I asked.

"Because you could see us, we have great interest in beings that can see us. If you can see us then maybe you can communicate with us. As you can see we were right."

"Sorry for shining my light at you."

It seemed a little light hearted now. "Don't worry about it. We understand and accept it as part of our life. You almost got me a number of times."

"Knowing I did that and knowing you now I feel a little guilty. I never intended to harm anyone."

"You didn't. We understood you were a child and children of all species cannot be held accountable for their actions. In most cases they are a reaction and it's not a deliberate act."

I was beginning to understand. "OK, where are we. I think we were talking about the number of weapons you would need."

They then began to describe what they had done and what they needed. "At this time we have the Devourers confined to a specific area. They have not developed the power needed to overcome our control, but from time to time they are able to temporarily get out of the controlled area."

"Just as they did last week?" I replied.

"Yes, just as they did your last week, as you called it."

"So, how many weapons?"

"We have a problem there Carl."

"And, what is that? And by the way do you have a name or something you are called?"

"Please call me Ho. We on the black side cannot determine how to tell you an

349

amount. To us I see you and that is a deth. Let me check in your mind. To us your one is the same as your thousand. There is no meaning in this term for us."

Things were starting to be complex. "Oh boy, this is going to be a problem. How am I going to determine what you need when you cannot relate to me a number? Let's start this way. What is a number? A number is a form of communications through mathematics. It is considered a universal language."

"Except for us?" Ho replied.

"Yeah, I guess so. OK, let's do it this way. You can see me, right?"

"Yes you are standing right in front of me."

"Do you see any other light sider being here?"

"No." Ho replied.

"OK, with just me present that is one. I am one single light being. If you saw another light being beside me or with me that would be two. Another would be three. Got it?

"Tell all the black side beings in this room to stand still. OK, I count twelve of you here right now. Does that help?"

There was a pause. "Yes, now we know what you are talking about. When you see just me as a black side being that means you see just me and that would be a "deth", if there is another with me that is a "seth" and then a "qeth" and so on."

After several minutes of being educated in their numbering system I figured out a way to determine the number of weapons they would need. In our terms, they needed around twenty-five thousand weapons. God, where was I going to get that number?

We agreed to meet again the next night, only this time it would be in my work shop at my home. I asked if they knew how to get there. "We are already there. We have been with you for many multiples."

"OK, I'll talk to you then and hopefully I'll have an answer for you at that time."

Where the hell was I going to get twenty-five thousand weapons let alone one? I had twenty-four hours to do this or at least come up with a plan and answer. On my way home I stopped at the store. My wife had asked that I pick up some milk. I almost forgot about it.

As I walked through the store to get the milk my mind was plowing through the means by which I was going to be able to supply the needed weapons to my counterpart on the black side. For some strange reason I trusted it and knew what it said was true. After all, Dave paid a heavy price to get my attention and bring me to this point.

I had retrieved the milk and was standing at the checkout line when it hit me. Have you ever had that feeling all your problems had just been answered and you had done absolutely nothing to achieve the means by which the solution came?

Well it happened to me. As I stood there I was looking at the display. You know, those display shelves that are at each checkout stand with different items you really don't want, but just in case you may.

My eyes settled on a small cylindrical item hanging from a peg on a small chain. I stopped, focused and just stood there staring at it. It dawned on me that it was a laser, one of those small low powered laser pointers. That was it. Light in its most concentrated form. I almost lost control of myself. People were starting to stare at me. I grabbed half a dozen of the pointers, paid for everything and got the hell out of there.

Let see, fifty-nine cents apiece times twenty-five thousand that come to just under fifteen thousand dollars, fourteen thousand seven hundred fifty dollars to be exact. Where the hell was, I going to get fifteen thousand dollars to buy a bunch of laser pointers? Crap, the dark side was waiting and depending on me coming through for them. I knew that I had to have a supply of these lasers by tomorrow evening, so I set my mind on finding a supplier and getting the units orders. I would do that first thing in the morning.

I guess the bigger issue was how I was going to explain a fifteen thousand dollar expense to my wife, especially when I failed to consult her about it. That would have to come later on. Right now I needed to get those items and get them to where ever they needed to be.

The next day I found a store that had the needed pointers in stock. It was a small store, named Duker's, and I was surprised that it carried the number of lights I needed, but they were there waiting for me. These were a little more powerful than the ones I had found, but their cost was less because of the volume purchase I was making. I ran to the

353

bank and got the needed funding and closed the deal.

Banks can be so accommodating. I figured it would be a week or two to make the loan. No problem. They were looking for loan applicants and just about hog tied me to try and give me more than I needed. I still had to explain it to Jane and that was going to be a problem I had not figured a way through that yet.

Do you know how many boxes make up twenty-five thousand laser pens? Well it was a few more than I had planned on, two hundred fifty to be exact. I had them delivered that afternoon and knew full well when the semi pulled up out front and started unloading the boxes into our garage, I had better be ready to explain things to Jane and fast. What I finally decided was that I had to tell her the truth and that was going to be a hard one, without her wanting me committed to an institution.

Well, we got past the unloading and that took until almost six thirty that evening. Jane restrained herself while the delivery people were there and then it hit the fan. I took her into the living room and we sat down and I then explained what was going on. I'll give her credit, she listened until I had finished and then came off the wall at me.

"You're crazy as hell. What is going on? Has Dave's death hit you that hard?"

I let her rave for a few minutes and then I asked her if she was through? That set her off for another ten minutes and by the end of that time period it was time to blow her mind.

"OK hon. you want to know what is going on and I can now tell you. Will you come into my shop with me now?"

"Carl, what is this all about?"

"Jane, I am going to tell you, but I need to show you as well. Please honey, you must trust me this one more time."

I stood up and she followed suit. As we came to the shop door I told her to stand back from the door and simply wait. She did as I told her and I opened door. It took several seconds for our eyes to adjust, but as they did I could see him there in the dark. I looked to Jane watching for the reaction I needed to insure that she was in fact seeing that figure in the dark. She was.

"What the hell is that?" She almost screamed.

I reached out and took her hand and told her to stop and get control of herself.

"Now Jane what you are going to hear and see is real. Be patient and understand you are not in danger here."

She looked at me with a completely lost look on her face. "Carl, is that actually something there? Am I seeing a real thing or something?"

"Yes hon. you are. We're about to step into the black side. It is an existing universe that runs parallel with our light-based universe and there are beings who live there. They have lived next to us from the beginning of time only we were not able to see them unless they wanted us to.

"Now we are going to step into their universe for a few minutes. It will feel no different to us other than being dark. What I want you to do is reach out with your hand into the darkness on the other side of the door, can you do that?"

Jane stepped closer to the door and raised her hand and started to push it through and into the darkness. I felt her grip on me increase and I increased mine on hers to let her know I was there.

I felt the contact when it reached out and touched her hand. She stopped and looked at her arm and then to me. "It's such a strong and soft touch."

With that we stepped into the darkness. It asked her if she was alright and she nodded her head. It then told her what was happening and I was helping them solve the problem that had resulted in Dave's death. I heard her say, "The children?"

The creature immediately told her not to worry. They had already placed a protection unit around our children and nothing could get at them. "In a few minutes you will be reunited with them, but now you need to know all the details as to what was about to happen and then they could start the engagement with the Devourers."

After about a half hour of laying out their tactics Jane and I were taken to the boy's bedroom. We could hear their breathing as we entered the room and they immediately cried out to Jane, "Mommy what is it?"

She sat down with them and told them they were angels there to help and protect them. I felt a surge in the darkness. "What is that?"

Ho told me the units that were there knew of our belief in angels and when she referred to them in that way, they became more determined to protect this woman and her children. "They will die to the being to protect them now. Yet, we need to make a backup plan just in case they cannot provide the level of protection that may be needed. You need to pick a place in the house where you can build a light shield for her and the children.

"Light shield?" I asked.

"Yes, a place where they can sit on the floor and have a number of light generators on the floor around them. All she need do is sit the children down and turn the light generators on and they will be protected. The generators must last for at least twice a qeth of your hours."

What followed next was a melee of activity. I ran to the store and found a dozen high intensity lamps and brought them back and set them up on the kitchen floor. We handed out the weapons to the units, two each and then started the disbursement to the action positions of the units that would carry out the attack against the Devourers. All was ready by midnight.

We told Jane she had to stay in that bedroom with the boys until such time the leader of the unit told her to get out or flee. At that point and only then was she to take the boys out of the bedroom and into the kitchen and start the light shield and then stay put. Do not vary from this plan, no matter what. It will be your only way of surviving this thing. She understood and got herself ready. We kissed and said our goodbye and then I had to leave.

As we moved off and back into my shop, I noticed there was a lot of activity going on around us. The place was full of movement, much of which I could not see any detail other than just knowing things were happening. Ho told me at this time we were about to attack the Devourers and that the next few hours in our time system would be extremely brutal. They handed me two lasers. "Are you ready?"

"Yeah, let's do it."

At that moment I felt him touch my upper arm and then the floor left me. We were moving through air, space, or whatever, but we were no longer in my shop. It's black and I can't see anything. As I said before in the dark there are differences in the density of objects with mass as they move around in the darkness and I could see there was a lot of movement. But, beyond that I could see nothing.

It was then I saw the first laser discharges start to take place. It started off to my left and then like a fire running through dry grass it spread. Lasers seemed to be going off all over the place. At first it looked haphazard, but then a pattern began to appear.

They were concentrating to both the left and right and moving in toward the middle. As the lasers moved toward the middle the number of units firing increased until it was just a mass of narrow red beams slicing through the darkness and hitting huge dark shadows.

As the intensity grew I could see the size and shape of the creatures they were shooting at. The first thing that entered my mind was that of an octopus. They had tentacle or arms. Not eight, but more like ten or twelve and they were big, probably twice the size of the largest of the dark creature that were attacking them. They threw themselves at the line of lasers and I saw a few go down.

It had turned into a pitch battle and I had no idea who had the upper hand at that point. Just then something grabbed me around the chest and I felt the arms wrapping around me. The pressure was extreme with the first contact. I knew then what Dave had gone through and all I could think of was Jane and the kids. Just then a mass of lasers hit this thing from every direction.

For the first time I saw what must have been a face. It was not a face as you would think, but an open hole in the middle of the massive head of this thing. I knew that in that hole was my death and it was coming down on me.

A second volley hit it and it spun around and at the same time let go of me and sent me sailing across whatever it was I was in. Just then I hit something hard and flat. It gave way and flew open and I went falling out onto the floor of a large open air mall. People around the door I came through stopped short and looked at me. Through the door I had just come flying through they could see all the lasers that were going off in there. They scattered like flies.

I heard the sound of a police siren followed by the arrival of a patrol unit. I was still trying to regain my orientation when the patrol car pulled up. When I saw it I almost vomited. It was a French police car. "What the hell." I was in France. "How could that be?"

Just then I felt it calling me to get back into the room and get the door shut. The officers were running toward me as I staggered back to the door and stepped inside. Ho immediately grabbed me and we were spinning away from the door and back into the battle. The first officer got to the door just as a black flash went off. It knocked him down and the flash radiated out over the top of him.

I remember seeing his face as the flash of blackness came out of the room and out over the mall area. It must have covered at least a hundred feet. As the flash dissipated it drew the door shut leaving two stunned officers lying on the mall floor wondering what had just happened.

By this time the battle was almost over. The attacking forces were mopping up the last two Devourers as Ho took me by the arm and started back to my shop. Somehow we had traveled half way around the world to France to fight a war that meant the survival of the world, both the black side and the light side, and now I was heading home. For the second time since this thing started my mind turned to Jane and the boys.

"Are they alright?" I asked.

"Yes, they are fine. One Devourer got through and the unit made quick work of it. Our forces are covering the entire black side universe at this time to make sure none have survived."

As we entered the bedroom Jane and the boys could not control themselves and they ran to me. The unit opened up for them and we held onto each other for what seemed like an hour. They told us to go back to our living room in the light and relax and they would be in contact again in a short time.

Once in our living room and we had calmed down, there was a knock on the front door. As I opened the door I found Detective James standing there. "Carl, what's going on here?"

"What do you mean detective?"

He was looking at me and he meant business. "Carl, we have gotten no less than a dozen calls of something going on here in your house, noise of every kind. The first officers to come here knocked and banged on the door and tried to gain entry only to find that they could not budge the doors or get any windows open. It was black as spades in here. Carl, what is going on?"

I could see that he was not going away without an answer. "Detective, would you please come and sit down and I will tell you everything."

After Detective James sat down I introduced my wife and boys and then asked if they would go to the family room and wait there. "Detective, there has been something going on here that I don't think you or anyone else will ever believe, but I'm going to tell you anyway. I know who, better yet, what killed Dave and the other victim."

"You do?"

"Yes, and you're not going to believe it, but before this night is over you will. Detective have you ever been afraid of the dark?"

A strange look came across his face. "That's a strange question."

"Yeah, it is, but please answer it for me and be patient."

He then nodded. "Yes, I was terribly afraid of the dark as a child."

"Why were you afraid of the dark?" I asked.

He thought for a moment. "Well, I would lay there at night and swear I could see things moving around in the dark, just outside of my reach. My dad would belittle me and call me dumb. Mom would just tell me it was my imagination."

"Was it?"

"I don't think so."

"Well detective I am here to tell you that what you thought you saw was in fact true."

"What?" His head jerked back as he looked at me.

I calmly continued. "That's right. They do live in the darkness. They call it the black side. They are real and they do come in contact with us often. We live in two parallel universes, one black and the other light. It was from this black side that the killer of Dave and the other victim came from. They are called Devourers and they have worked for centuries trying to develop a means of getting at us, to feed on us.

"The other beings of the black side have been victimized by these creatures for all time. Once they broke through the contact barrier the others from that side knew they had to do something to stop them. With that they contacted me. The rest I think you know about. I bought twenty-five thousand laser pens as weapons that would kill the Devourer and they worked.

"A battle was fought across the face of the earth this night. Only it was fought in the other black side universe. It did spill over into the light side and that is what you got the calls for.

If you check with the French police they will have a record of a stranger falling through a mall door onto the floor of an open air mall and then having a huge black cloud flow out over the mall and then flash back in and through the door taking the stranger with it. That sir was me and I had almost been killed by one of the Devourers." I stopped to let him think.

"Carl, I don't know if this story will fly back at the office."

I felt myself smile. "I know detective so I have made arrangements for you to meet my counterpart on the black side."

That stopped him cold. A real look of fear swept across his face. "What?"

I reassured him that it was all right. "Yes, if you're willing you can meet him right now and get the rest of your questions answered.

"First I need to caution you. They do not communicate as you would expect, it's all mental. They speak to your mind. Understand?"

He was nodding again. "Yes. OK, let's go."

As we approached my shop door I felt Detective James stiffen up, his hand moved oh so slightly toward his gun. "Detective, no guns, you are not in danger; I can assure you of that."

His hand relaxed and I opened the door. We stood there for several seconds until his eyes adjusted to the dark and then he saw it. At first he started to back off, but I took hold of his elbow and held him in place.

"Take your time and clear your mind. When you're ready let me know and we will step inside."

As with my wife I had him reach out through the door first and let Ho take hold of his hand. His reaction was the same and we stepped in. For the next two hours the detective learned of every detail of the past three weeks including the death of Dave and the other and the battle that had just been fought.

Believe it or not, I was declared a liberator in their universe and a special recognition was given me. My sons were given a permanent unit to oversee them the rest of their lives. And my wife and I were given free passage to any place on the face of the world at no cost to us. If we wanted to spend a weekend in Hawaii, we walked through the shop door and out onto a beach or veranda somewhere on Hawaii, of our choice. What a way to travel.

The families of the victims, Dave's family and the other were not left out. The black flash device that the Devourers had developed and used was given to the families. They receive working models of the Black Flash unit which were used to demonstrate to the government and several arms companies. The resulting deal ended with both families receiving twenty-five million dollars each, after taxes and were ensured a good life from then on.

The companies were amazed at the device. The demo unit was dropped in an open field that was at least a mile and a half across and when it went off it sent a black cloud over half the area. It completely blacked out the area and then slowly dissipated. They found that if they had personnel in the area wearing infrared glasses when it went off they could see any being clearly and precisely. It was a perfect raid and apprehension tool. Many lives would be saved by its use in the future.

Well, there you have it. Never underestimate nature. What your mind and senses may detect may seem impossible, but you never know. If anyone tells me there is nothing in the dark, I simply smile and think to myself, if you only knew…

By this time Frank was standing and moving around behind the counter. He pulled out a bag and opened a couple of drawers and started taking things out and placing them in the bag. He looked at me. "These are some personal items I wish to take with me in my retirement. You wouldn't get any use out of them and frankly they would mean little or nothing to you.

He finished filling the bag and then walked back around the counter and stood in front of me. He took my arm and turned me toward the back room and we walked back to the door and he opened it. We stepped into the back room and then he turned to me.

"Delbert, you will do a fine job here at Duker's Store. Remember to stay relaxed and don't get involved with the people that come in the door. It's their lives that are bringing them here for whatever it is they need. What results from their coming here is for them and them alone and does not involve you.

"All you do is supply their need, whatever that may be. After that it's wherever their lives are taking them which will happen and you have no part of it. Once they're done with the item it will return to its rightful place for storage, and remain there.

"For the perishable items, they will come and get them and then you have no further concern for whatever the item or items were.

"Delbert, you provide a service. You are not a judge of others actions. They will come in here from the past and the present and the future. Sometimes you will know the difference but it is not your place to address their time and actions. Just provide whatever it is they need and leave it at that."

I stood there looking at him and then it came to me. "Frank, I don't understand one thing. In the past this store was turned over to a blood relative. I don't think I'm one of your relatives."

He turned back to me and reached out and put his hand on my shoulder. "Delbert, I can assure you that you are a blood relative. Your great grandfather, who was my father's brother and my uncle, had a son and that son had a son and that son had a daughter who gave birth to you out of wedlock and was forced by her parents to put you up for adoption. She did as she was told and from that moment on, until now, none of the family knew where you went or whether you were alive or dead.

"Yes Delbert, you are a blood relative and one that deserves this position above all the other blood relatives because you are the closest to me in our relationship.

"Now take over the store and enjoy the adventure you are about to set out on. This is your life now Delbert and you will live it here in Duker's Store until the day you determine it is time for you to retire."

"But Frank, I couldn't be your nephew, you're one hundred eighty-nine years old and that would make my mother even older if she were alive today. No Frank that is impossible, you have to be mistaken."

371

He smiled and set the backpack down and walked over to a desk by the door to the storage room and opened a drawer. "Delbert, this is the story of our family and the blood line of the Duker's. You read that story and it will explain everything to you concerning your blood line and heritage. I can assure you that you and I are family. He then reached down and picked his bag up and when he stood up, I saw he was about my height with red hair and green eyes, just like me.

I was stunned as I stood there looking at him. "How come I didn't see the resemblance until now?"

"Because, Delbert, you weren't supposed to see it until now."

At that he turned and walked back toward the back areas of the back room. I watched as he walked away from me and after about a half hour he slipped out of sight.

I was now alone in the Store and the sole employee and servant to all those who come here to Duker's Store. Just then I heard a car pulling into the parking spot in front of the store and I walked out to meet my first customer.

"Welcome to Duker's Store, how may I help you?"